TO GIVE TO THE LIGHT

a
biographical
novella

MICHAEL A. DIMARCO

Readers' Comments

"Michael DiMarco has been a vital force in international journalism for decades, but *To Give To The Light* elevates him in importance and gives us all a family saga confronting one of the often misunderstood yet shouted about issues in today's American politics: immigration. It doesn't matter where or when your family came to America, this is a universal tale about us — and you."

➥ **James Grady,** creator of *Condor* and author of 2025's critically anticipated novel *American Sky*.

"DiMarco's novel is a delightful and evocative read. It relates the life story of his grandfather who grew up in Italy and emigrated to the United States in 1913. The novel provides a rich, detailed account of his grandfather's life, focusing primarily on his family's relationships. These relationships are the stuff of everyday life, but they make up a tale that is both interesting and moving. In addition, the novel shows the reader the beauty and value of discovering intimate details in his or her own ancestors' stories. Without such personal tidbits, the idea of heritage remains a rather abstract concept that barely extends beyond a flow chart or family tree. DiMarco's novella is just the opposite: it is full of vignettes of his grandfather's story. Moreover, the tale has worldwide applicability, as the protagonist is an ordinary man with an ordinary story. This aspect enables the novella to universalize the immigrant experience, ensuring that it will be of interest to anyone who has an ancestor with a journey, whether that journey began in Italy or somewhere else."

➥ **Raymond LaVerghetta, Ph.D.** Immediate Past President, Abruzzo and Molise Heritage Society, Washington, D.C.

"Back in the day, you didn't need a writer to know the family stories; you simply needed regular family interaction and a good memory. Things have changed, and through writers like Michael DiMarco, we can know not only the history of the DiMarco family, but the history that surrounds stories that relate to all of us who descend from immigrants. *To Give to the Light* is a great testament to what can be accomplished with applying imagination to family history. Well researched and clearly presented, the novella captures the experience of 20th century Italian immigration to the United States in a way that will resonate in us all."

➡ **Fred L. Gardaphé, Ph.D.** Distinguished Professor of Italian American Studies Queens College, CUNY and the John D. Calandra Italian American Institute.

"Behind every person, a story is to be found, and DiMarco's story is another piece of the invisible human puzzle, called immigration. In some ways, all immigrants share some ancestral feelings about leaving their homeland and starting anew in a foreign country. It is a journey back in time, where two realities collide, the village's life in the Italian south, and the new life in America. Michael DiMarco's novella is about one story, one voice among millions of others, but it is the voice of all immigrants."

➡ **Renato Ventura, Ph.D.** Associate Professor, Global Languages and Culture, University of Dayton

Cover design by
Via Media Publishing Company
Image created using openart.ai
image_538YOELv_1715984886706_raw.jpg

ISBN 979-8-218-49025-6

Dedication
Appreciation to the immigrants from
Montenero Val Cocchiara (IS), Italy,
and others who have faced similar
life experiences in selfless ways.

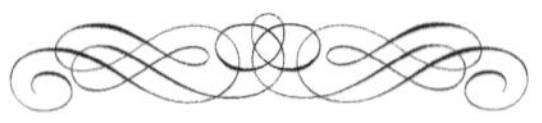

Table of Contents

chapter 1

To Give to the Light
dare alla luce

The mayor, Angelo DiFiore, arrives at our home just in time to witness the birth of my fourth offspring. Pressed by the contractions occurring in rhythm with my wife, Antonia's, breaths, its tiny body has started to emerge inch by inch from the womb into this world. It's nerve-racking knowing of the large number of stillbirths in the village. Giulia, my sister, gently wipes trickling sweat from my wife's brow as Carmela, the midwife, attentively receives the newborn. Seeing a healthy boy emerge, joyous tears flood my eyes. The baby's cry is sweetly delicate yet shows signs of strength. Cradling the baby with both hands, Carmela places him into the arms of my smiling Antonia who radiates a loving bond. I'm torn between the bliss of having a fourth son and being anxious for his future living in this Italian region of Molise.

I step in close to the bed and lean over, brush strands of Antonia's silky black hair away to kiss her forehead. We had previously decided that, if God gives us a boy, we'd name him Michele, after Antonia's father. I want to remember all about this special day—July 17, 1893—as the warm summer afternoon air floats into our mountain village from the valley below. It brings the fragrance of the cut straw drying in the fields. As I'm sensing the surroundings of the moment, the mayor breaks the silence by making an announcement.

"Congratulations, dear Antonia and Serafino DiMarco! With Michelino's arrival, the population of Montenero Val Cocchiara is now exactly two thousand! It took one thousand years from the village's birth to this day to reach this high mark. The few original settlers came to this area to work the fields and tend the animals, adding to the stability of the nearby Abbey of San Vincenzo. They built simple, one-room wooden homes along the swamp in the valley, but today we have these strong stone houses on this *monte nero*, 'black mountain' top, where Michelino will enjoy the grand vistas of the central Apennine Mountains."

The midwife allows a few female relatives and friends of Antonia to enter the room. Mayor DiFiore tugs at my shirt sleeve to lead me out the door. We stroll fifteen minutes along the cobblestone street and arrive at a cantina filled with friends waiting to celebrate the birth of my son. As my foot lands on the cantina's threshold, there is a roar: "Toast to Papa Serafino!" A hundred glasses point toward me, filled to their brims with Chianti or marsala. Shots will soon follow of sambuca, and Martini and Rossi vermouth.

"All my friends! Antonia and I thank you from our hearts! My newly arrived son, Michelino, would like to drink with you too. And to show his appreciation, he would drink *waaaay* too much, then he would surely piss on all of you!" The crowd expects such village humor and responds in kind.

The cantina owner questions, "And the father? I hear the baby looks like Bobo, the village idiot!"

A roar of laughter fills the room. Before the chuckling stops, even my brother Donato proclaims:

"Better to look like Bobo, than inherit Serafino's baboon face!"

"Serafino, did you count all his toes?" asks the cheese maker.

One of the more vulgar members of the party quips, "With a newborn, there's no place for your head to rest on Antonia's milk-laden breasts!" He's quick to add a more amicable sentiment: "But, you can be free to spend more time with us, bullshitting around the card table playing scopa with our marked cards!"

The eating, drinking, and joking continue until closing time. It's late Monday evening. Tomorrow is another workday. We depart the cantina in good spirits and stagger to our homes under the light of a nearly full moon. We must wake in the morning with the roosters' crow to tend the land and animals. We work from dawn to dusk almost every day.

I return home and, under the dim glow of an oil lamp, see Antonia asleep with Michele by her side. Her slumber is well deserved following eight hours of labor. Carmella the midwife is awake in a rocking chair. My three-year-old son, Pasquale, is sleeping in her arms. She looks exhausted too. I switch places with her so she can return home. My sisters-in-law, Angela and Domenica, leave too. Only my sister Giulia stays. She will help us out, being attentive to Antonia and the children. Five of my seven siblings are female. I can comfortably rely on two of them to help until Antonia feels strong enough to return to her normal routine.

• • •

FIFTEEN YEARS LATER

When any villager has a medical problem, the doctor will listen with a stethoscope to their chest or back, asking the patient to say *trenta-tre*, thirty-three—the age when Jesus died on the cross. When Michele was born, I was thirty-three years old. Now I'm forty-eight. I must stay healthy and strong for many more years to help the growing family. Love for Antonia and the children gives me strength and energy. Often, I mull over the family's future. Is this the best place to raise a family? What does the village and land here offer? How can I best provide for all my children? Although I am constantly anxious with such thoughts, with God's grace I have hope for my children.

Since our marriage nineteen years ago—it was on September 21 I must remember—we've had the same daily routine. Our activities are as predictable as sunrise and sunset. We're village folk, tied to the land and its rhythms. We tend animals and fields. Plus, we're raising seven children. The only real breaks we get from the humdrum come with the holidays and Sundays—the day of rest.

Our marriage almost didn't occur. In a village of two thousand inhabitants, it isn't easy to find a spouse. Usually, eligible prospects are introduced through family members and sometimes to potential partners from nearby villages. Groups of females would walk an hour or two to sell eggs in nearby villages like Alfedena to make some money, while keeping an eye open for available bachelors.

My Antonia was born here in Montenero, but before we seriously dated, we had to learn if we were related in any way. Both of us have the same surname, DiMarco, which is a common family name here in Molise. Some are related and some aren't. Since Montenero is under the religious administration of the Bishop of Trivento, His Holiness verified that our bloodlines are distant enough that we were free to marry. Ever since being united in matrimony we've faced each new day together.

Although our daily activities are predictable, we always find that our conversations are richly engaging. I usually return home after the workday to a hot dinner lovingly prepared by Antonia's hands. She often knows what will be served days in advance, baking bread for the week, trading with others for items like wine, cheese, or sausage. Sitting at the dinner table with her and the children is a time of great joy of togetherness. We relax while hearing the daily recap of each individual. A son caught a frog in the Zittola River. Our girl sewed a button on her shirt. The sheep shears broke. We laugh at the baby's mispronunciation of *farfalla* (butterfly), saying *fafafa*. As parents, we often offer words of encouragement as well as humorous conversations about our personal quirks.

After the children are asleep, Antonia and I get into bed and talk on the more important topics, such as our finances and work priorities, but mostly about the children. The eldest, Giuseppe and Carmine, have minds of their own already. Stubborn minds. But they do work hard. Michele and Pasquale have matured quickly over the past fifteen years. They are a great help in raising their three younger siblings, Elvira, Filippo, and Vincenzo.

"Pasquale takes after you, Antonia. In so many ways, he's a mommy's boy. He's fine-featured and well-mannered. He dotes on the young ones. Seems he is trying to help them mature quickly, but he still reverts to childish play under their influence."

"Yes," responds Antonia. "He's quite a gentleman for a seventeen-year-old. And hardworking too, much like Michele. Even though Michele is two years younger, he appears to be older than Pasquale because he's inherited your broad chest and brawn. Jackets and long-sleeved shirts are never long enough in length for your arms. Cuffs fall two or three inches short of your wrists. Yes, you're right, Pasquale takes after me, but Michele is your duplicate."

These two boys are a blessing. I hate to bring up to Antonia the fact that the other children exhibit some of the more common adolescent behaviors. "Maybe we spoiled the older boys, Giuseppe and Carmine. They always put themselves first. With only one point of view, they argue with everyone and anyone. Elvira is feisty. I'd say she has a short fuse, but it seems she has no fuse! Perhaps she had some trauma learning that my papa died less than a month after she was born? The other three boys are energetic, like little tornados running around the house. I praise your saintly patience with them, my dear."

Antonia doesn't take all the credit, saying, "I'm happy my sister and your sister come to help almost every day. They are so thoughtful, making the effort to be with us and ease the daily burdens. It gives us time together to chat and get work done, like crocheting sweaters or mixing cornmeal."

There is a pause in our conversation. Antonia turns toward me and places a hand on my chest. She turns onto her side, curling her left leg around my left leg. Then, in an alluring whisper, she asks, "Honey, are you tired?"

After twenty years of marriage, I understand and smile at her way of hinting. Every day I feel her loving presence as our lives revolve around each other. But at times when we embrace, it seems we really are one, knowing what each other thinks and feels without saying any words.

Through the seasons, Antonia and I witness the rapid maturity of our four elder boys. Realistically, they are no longer "our little boys," but are young men.

Plowing under the autumn sun's rays, I pause the horses to wipe sweat off my brow. I yell across the furrows: "Antonia! All well?"

"Yes! Yes! The boys are keeping up throwing seeds and helping me rake."

"I will give each a turn at guiding the plowshare."

During the harvest, an army of men swing the long scythes in a steady rhythm. They produce a melodic hum by sliding their sharpening stones back and forth across the five-foot blades. Wheat falls neatly to the ground to be gathered for threshing. This is extremely hard work, callusing hands, tightening arm muscles. Pasquale and Michele keep pace without complaint. Giuseppe and Carmine march to their own drum, often out of rhythm with the others.

Seems the elder two boys have stopped learning. They aren't open to conversation and alternate perspectives. Pasquale and Michele have learned almost all I could teach them for life in the village. They have mastered using the common tools, including sheep shears, mason chisels, and woodworking tools. Both know every type of animal on our lands, domestic and wild, and how they harmonize nature's balance and benefit the villagers. They are also acutely aware of the dangers that can appear: vipers, wolves, wild boars, or brown bears.

Under their hands, the family garden is miraculous, producing a variety of vegetables and herbs. They also know how to prepare and use more than fifty herbs for medical use for people as well as for our animals, especially horses, pigs, sheep, and cows. Pasquale favors working with cows, regularly doing the milking. He also enjoys making caciocavallo and scamorza cheese.

Farming, gardening, fishing, milling grain, cooking, bathing … almost everything we do in the village relies on water. The valley is blessed with the Zittola River. However, for home life, our source of water is the natural spring that continuously flows on the south edge of the village. For convenience, a large stone fountain was built there in 1821 with four spigots where the cool fresh water falls into a trough.

Antonia alerts me, "Serafin', we are out of water for cooking, cleaning, and bathing! The barrels are empty. Do you have time to go to the fountain to refill them?"

I balance two empty barrels on the sides of our donkey and head down the hill on Via Fonte. At the fountain, others are filling their oak wood barrels or large clay jars. Horses and sheep are drinking nearby. Women are washing clothes, repeatedly beating the fabric over smooth stones. The fountain area is one of the more active spots in Montenero because of its practical importance as well as it being conducive to socializing.

While I wait for my turn to get to a spigot, I chat with a few of them, who were discussing their daily lives and the ancestral lineages that go back over centuries. Two ladies balance their filled clay jars on top of their heads and start their walk back home. A weathered elder lifts his full barrel onto a donkey and departs.

Village life has not changed much since antiquity. While my two barrels are under the spigots, my mind wonders. Should my children remain in Montenero? What are the reasons to continue living here?

As it has been for Montenerese over the centuries, I realize the greatest blessing for my children

is the *pantano*, the vast swamp-
land in the valley just a twenty-
minute walk from our homes.
All the associated attributes
show how unique this place is as
a geographic wonderland and
how fortunate we are to live
here.

During much of the year
the flat valley is relatively dry,
except for the Zittola River that
traverses the area lengthwise.
Whenever the river overflows,
the land gets submerged, occurring most notably during the
spring thaw. This vast plain—
about three miles long and as

wide as a half mile at one end—gives ample room for
hundreds of horses and cattle to graze. It's shaped
like a long-handled spoon: a spoon-shaped valley, a
val cocchiara, surrounded by karst hills.

In the pantano, the children particularly love
catching the variety of colorful butterflies. By the
sudden outbursts of vocal rejoicing in the valley, we
can guess a prized winged insect was caught. Who
can count the over one hundred types of these delicate
winged creatures? By the riverbank, children often
catch trout and eels by hand. A high-pitched shriek
can indicate that one of the boys caught an eel and
threw it at a girl as a sign of flirtation ... The youngsters play just as we did when we were their age.

The abundant variety of flowers adds a colorful
spectrum to the area. I've heard that there are nearly
three thousand kinds. Most of the children are still

too young to realize how fortunate they are to live in this natural paradise.

For leisure, adults sometimes hike into the surrounding mountains. While walking, one is soon surrounded by trees, such as the flowering ash and maple. At higher elevations, oak, silver fir, and beech change the scenery. Snow can outline the highest mountains well into the summer months. By ascending the high peaks, one is rewarded with spectacular views of Montenero in the distance.

Overhead may be seen the majestic golden eagle, but flights of sparrow hawks and martins are more common. Migratory birds arrive even from distant Africa. Along the river are often gray herons and wagtails. Amid all this vegetation, hikers spot foxes, deer, and the large mountain hare. Yes, my boys have intimately learned all about this terrain and what plants and animals live here.

Among the abundant gifts nature provides for the Montenerese are the noble Pentro horses. They are our pride, grazing by the hundreds in the pantano. This unique breed originated here a few thousand years ago, useful for their meat, pulling heavy loads, riding, or to be admired for their beauty. Certainly, our cows, sheep, and goats are important, but the Pentro is symbolic of the independent character of the people in this region.

Michele has a special aptitude for handling horses. Most of the horses here are wild, but Michele talks with them, brushes their manes, feeds them … There is one horse nobody else can sit upon except Michele. He named it Gaius after Gaius Pontius the Samnite commander who defeated the Romans in battle. More inspiring than a Trojan horse, the fifteen-hands-high, 875-pound Pentro stallion does not become agitated whenever Michele mounts him. Together their posture gives an impression of a Caesar riding bareback.

Besides the bounty of nature, what is here for my children? How will they grow up in this village? In future years, will their lives improve or turn worse? At present, we are living on the edge. We aren't rich by any means. The established residents who own some land, a home, and perhaps animals, are doing fine. Our hand-me-down clothing may be tattered, but we have enough to eat and have shelter during the winters. Sure, there are some who go barefoot. The unfortunate need to beg for bread and the kindhearted help them. The seven mills here are always busy grinding. Antonia's fresh baked bread makes every dinner mouthwatering. Her polenta made with our homemade sausage and tomato sauce is always a welcomed standard dish.

It is our destitute who remain a concern, especially when there is a natural disaster, like a year with poor crops, an earthquake, or when a cholera epidemic hits as we had in 1854. But we manage. Our patron saint, Saint Clemente, brought here from Roman catacombs in 1776, looks over everyone, especially the faithful churchgoers. And the annual procession and bonfire on Saint Antonio's feast day in January ensures our animals stay healthy and provide for us.

Our hamlet is typical of the many villages dotting the south Italian countryside. In our region, one difference is whether a village is in the lower or higher elevations, closer to the Adriatic coast or amid the central mountain range. The mountain villages cling to the hilltop features. The walkways between the winding rows of gray limestone buildings offer some shelter when the weather turns windy. The central mountain locations were safer in the days when Muslim pirates attacked shoreline villages, porting away our brethren into slavery on the Barbary Coast in North Africa.

When walking through Montenero, a medieval pattern can be seen that indicates the defensive nature of the town. There was planning when it came to using the natural rock and the inclines of the hill. We often congregate in front of the municipal building where there is the *Porta Nova*, the New Gate, a passageway surrounded by fortified walls. There are a few secret passageways between buildings that were useful to escape from invaders, such as bandits who roamed the region.

Most homes here are small and of simple design. There are others that reflect the higher status of their occupants, such as the Duke's Palace at the top of Montenero in the area we call The Court. The palazzo dates back at least to the very early sixteenth century. More recent noble families, such as the Carafa, Sangro, and Caracciolo lived there until the eighteenth century.

The centuries-old Mannarelli family home that belonged to a "fabricator and tailor" has excellent highly decorative inscriptions carved into the walls surrounding the entrance: flowers, religious symbols, and perhaps scissors or a humorously placed phallic symbol? Nearby is the De Archangeles–Del Forno home, built in 1691, which houses an apothecary. The building's magnificently designed multi-arched foyer is set off by the heavy wooden double-door entrance. Locking the doors can be reinforced with a solid wooden beam. Above to the left of the entrance is a windowless gap through the wall, angled to the area in front of the doorway. If any unwelcomed visitors arrive, such as robbers, the opening brings them into clear view of rifle sights.

Another structure is impressive for its size: a multistory Renaissance-style building dating to 1751 and built by a family who made their fortune seasonally transporting sheep along the drovers' trails to and from the southern grazing plains each winter. It served as a hospital for some years, but today there are several families living there. The sick, infirm, and injured also find support in faith.

Small chapels are located on the village periphery acting as sacred sentinels. Saint Nicola of Bari was a very important church in early times, but today the Church of Saint Maria of Mount Carmel is more important. The real soul of today's village, Saint Maria of Loreto, the mother church, contains the relics of Saint Clemente. It was founded at the start of the fifteenth century. This is where we attend mass every Sunday. The choir loft is of ornate carved woods, including a bellows organ dating back to 1721. The altars date back to the sixteenth and seventeenth centuries. The white-washed stone floor dates from 1530. The artworks inspire. Silver crucifixes. Oil paintings. Baroque-style wooden doors. Multicolored marble inlays. Craftsmen from Naples, Sulmona, and Pescocostanzo created the best pieces.

Sometimes after mass, we go to the portico of seventeen arches on the side of the church facing the pantano. The magnificent vista offers a view over the rooftops toward the valley and surrounding hills and mountains. Next to the portico is a bell tower with the date of 1570 inscribed on its stone surface. Its present shape shows some recent repairs.

As I review the village as the birthplace of my children, I reflect on my days here as well as those of my parents. The DiMarco family roots reach back to at least 1753 as recorded in the detailed, handwritten land registry made under orders of King Charles with a goal to end feudalism. Perhaps the tax system was better then than now? A mid-fifteenth-century census record includes names common in Montenero today, but there's no mention of a DiMarco. Who really knows ancient ancestry? Either by divine providence or simple fate, we were born in this time and place. I can only think of the future and how it will be for the children.

chapter 2

Against Fate, Knowledge Is Useless
contro la fortuna, il sapere non giova

From any viewpoint in Montenero, no other village can be seen. Our village is surrounded by verdant mountains, seemingly secluded from the rest of Italy and the outside world. As a result, a sense of blessed tranquility can cuddle one's whole being. This is a false security. At times, thunderstorms roll over our village and into our valley, filling everyone with fear and terror. Storms are gathering and I look for shelter for my family.

"Serafino, you worry too much!" shouts Guido, the bartender in the cantina. "Don't forget the *Risorgimento*—our country's rising again! The Kingdom of Italy is still young and growing. The work of Mazzini, Cavour, and Garibaldi is coming to fruition ever since unification."

"Yes, when the Kingdom was created, I was one year old. During the so-called unification, there were revolts even here in Montenero! Hell, when our King Vittorio Emanuele II was escorted through Molise by the military, there were a dozen arrests of our own villagers ... Fabrizio, Danese, Del Forno, Ricchiuto, Tornincasa, and others. Charges against them were serious—charges of conspiracy, murder, vandalism, theft, and threats on lives. They preferred the French to rule over us rather than a northerner from the capital in Turin."

My good friend Nicola Scalzitti orders another round. While Guido pours, Nicola talks of Giuseppe Garibaldi, an independence fighter who returned from South America to help unite Italy. "The southern regions—the Kingdom of Two Sicilies—were in chaos under the Spanish and looking for a new ruler to bring stability to the regions. General Garibaldi and his thousand soldiers only needed to ask to take over the lands and give them to the King. They found great support among locals who were tired of chaos and the Garibaldini soldiers fought through weak opposition."

"You are right, Nicol'," I agree. "These major events are closest to our time, but much has happened before that has brought us here to the present. Our position in the southern half of the boot has always brought scars. How many times have the Germanic groups invaded and ruled here over the past two thousand years? The Visigoths, Vandals, Franks, Swabians? Hannibal led his soldiers and elephants over the Alps to our area, destroying our properties. Others came, including Attila the Hun!"

Nicola fills in additional history. "We see the influence in our land of the Lombards and Normans too. And later came invasions by the French, Spanish, and Austrians. Their castles are in each region—the Spanish fortress in L'Aquila and even nearby in Cerro a Volturno, Roccamandolfi, and Barrea. Some are in ruins, but many stand magnificently today like Svevo Castle in Termoli on the coast."

"And we can't leave out other invaders who came from the south," Guido remembers. "The Byzantines and the Arab Saracens. The Arabs burned, raped and robbed throughout Sicily and all the south. A thousand years ago, they destroyed the great Abbey at Castel San Vincenzo, killing some monks on the main altar. Ransacked. The famed religious complex is just walking distance from here. Montenero first appears because of the abbey's need for people to populate and cultivate their land and breed livestock, and to help protect the abbey from invaders."

I can't help but think about our origins in antiquity. "It seems we have been under the thumb, sword, or gun of others ever since the Samnite tribes were conquered by Rome over two thousand years ago. They were the last free people of this area. Our Pentro horses were here then. At least these regal animals retain some of the independent spirit."

Nicola nods in agreement, then strengthens the point. "Have you heard of the Samnite site found near Pietrabbondante? It was discovered about fifty years ago, although it's been there for over two thousand years. The drawings I've seen show a complex of various temples, statues, weapons, and the huge theater. The sacred location on a high hill overlooks hundreds of miles into the land of the Samnites. The setting seems to be a home for gods rather than mortals. A connection between earth and sky."

As more customers enter the cantina, Nicola and I retreat to a side table to continue our discussion, out of earshot of the others. There is an invisible threat of potential violence that radiates from irrational men with short tempers who have their own political views. We are careful with what we say even in hushed tones.

Nicola glosses over the centuries since our early Samnite tribes. "In every century, people in this area have had to assimilate to conquers. The most recent is the conquering of the south by the northerners. The northerners despise us. They certainly don't want to help us. It is easier just to kill or imprison us whenever there is an opportunity or ship us out far away from here."

"Nicol', millions of us southerners have left already, mostly to North and South America. The government's solution for the *southern problem* is to help us leave, as you say. Unlike so many others here, I have sympathy for the northerners. They are better organized, and cooperative compared to us. We're too emotional and hot-headed, don't you think? Geez, we can't even get along with each other. Look at the hostilities among the locals ..."

"Yes, Serafin'. I must agree with you on this. In addition to the centuries of foreign rule, perhaps it is the undercurrent here, the instinct to fight back, right or wrong. The numerous and constant revolts. The petty thievery and acts of violence against those with any opposing thought. We've had the infamous brigands roaming the land, attacking whoever they wished, whenever they wished. Killing and being killed in the most horrific ways. A brigand wrote on a large stone in the Abruzzo mountains: *'In 1820 was born Vittorio Emanuele II, the King of Italy. First was the Kingdom of Flowers. Now it is the Kingdom of Misery.'* How can we ignore this emotional under-current of hate and hopelessness? Blaiming others for our own problems? At the same time, what can we do to improve the south? Improve our own living conditions?"

"I don't know, Nicol'. The northerners don't know how to relate to southerners. Unfortunately, we have a difficult enough time dealing with ourselves. It seems we are pushing against overwhelming odds. Corruption is everywhere. As we speak, a delegate—selected by the province prefect—is here to manage our village on a temporary basis. This problem started in 1886! Back then, the provincial committee of Campobasso found irregularities and abuses in our administration. Just last year investigations were carried out to discern the problems and provide solutions. Twenty years have passed, and nothing has changed! Still there is negligence of the administrators, incompetence, and graft. Power is in the shadows. Secret societies have their own organization. We hear more and more about the growth and power of the Mafia."

"Oh, my dear friend Serafin', and where are we now? ... We're on a precipice facing the tides of European belligerents! Each country in competition with the others."

"You see it too, uh, Nicol'? The political powers in Turin chose to fight three wars with the Austrians, managing to retrieve some lands with Italian-speaking populations in the northeast. France helped, but politics shift like quicksand. The most powerful countries are seeking more power, more wealth, more land ... establishing colonies near and far, when possible, like Austro-Hungary ruling Bosnia and Herzegovina. We know how far-reaching the arms of other imperialist countries reached, be it Germany, France, Britain, or Spain. And the Kingdom of Italy feels it necessary to do the same. But Nicol', how will this situation help us, even in the long run?"

"Sorry to say, my friend, but I don't see any good coming from all this nationalistic pride. It is only leading to alliances and broken alliances, a political-military chess game in which we all will lose. Sorry to even speak of this. I fear for our families, especially for the innocent children."

"Even if we aren't in a position to comprehend the whole political arena, we are feeling the tensions. It's the main topic in conversations. It's front-page news and the focal point for scholars. Nicol', I must talk with my wife about this. This won't be easy on her. She's a mother. She won't like such a conversation. But millions have already left this 'paradise inhabited by devils,' as the northerners say about us. My four eldest are of age to make a move, start a new life elsewhere. I feel like I'm tearing off an arm to let them go."

The next morning Antonia lets me sleep in. Even the aroma of espresso doesn't wake me. When I do rise, I see she had gotten the younger children dressed and made them breakfast already. Except for the youngest, she added just a dash of strong coffee to their cups of hot milk, turning the white color to a creamy light tan. I stumble out of bed with a hangover and look like I've been dragged behind the plow across a rocky field. It's Sunday and I try my best to be sunny for the family. I wash my face, comb my hair, and go to the kitchen table.

"Buongiorno! How are all my angels this fine morning?!"

Antonia's omelet and freshly baked bread give me some comfort. I think of how the future of the family will change and can't help but feel an anxiety grip the fibers of my body.

Antonia and the elder boys realize I'm struggling to hide the throbbing pain from my night at the cantina. They don't know why I got into this condition. It's a state that is unusual for me, so they are curious, but refrain from asking.

Done with breakfast, Elvira washes most of the dishes and plays with her doll and the older boys go outside to meet friends. Carmine, the four-year-old, plays with a wooden toy I carved for him last weekend. Elvira leaves to meet a friend, taking Carmine with her. Now, Antonia starts asking why I'm so out of sorts.

We sit on the small outside balcony facing the valley, the morning sun's rays warming the skin. I start to repeat the main points from the previous night to lead up to the conclusion that our four eldest should emigrate. At that point, Antonia rises in a fury of protest! In our more than twenty years of marriage, I've never seen her act this way. It's like I just stabbed her in the heart. Jittery and crying, she dashes into the house to hide from the world. I try to put my arm around her, but she shrugs it off.

From across the room, I speak gently to her.

"Dear Antonia, there are so many benefits for our sons if they live abroad in a stable, prosperous country. We can keep in contact with them, writing letters. They will find good jobs and be able to visit us. Perhaps we will visit them too, or even move to their new country. They would be safe from the violence we too often see here. They can wear new clothes and have good shoes. No hand-me-downs. Above all, Antonia, I sense that all the political tensions here in Europe will erupt into war. Our sons would be drafted to fight so the north can prosper but, as southerners, they themselves would only sacrifice. If war does come, they may never return home."

She sits unresponsive, hunched over with her head in her hands, mumbling, "No. No. No." My presence now is just another pressure on her. I decide to go for a walk and let her calm down. I go to meet some friends, and we play cards on the outside veranda of a cantina at the base of the village. The talk at the table turns to emigration. Others are thinking the same way and are making plans to leave or to let their children leave for lands of opportunity. We are all under the same enormous weight.

Two hours later, I return home to find Antonia fidgeting by cleaning the house while talking with my sister Giulia. When she sees me enter, she looks at me in silence, drops her towel on the table, and comes to me with a big hug, placing her head against my chest.

"Sorry, my love. I know you wish the best for all the family. To see the boys leave to a foreign country, is almost as bad a death. But it is not death. We can bear it. I too want to see them happy and safe."

"We will begin to feel some happiness for them once they settle," I whisper in her ear. "We'll hear of their progress and know they are safe. You have a mother's love. It is strong, supported and enhanced by your emotions. I should have expected you to protest. Only a cold-hearted person would not do that. Your love will give them strength to take the ship, learn the language, and work hard to build their lives ... and to give us grandchildren!"

"My Serafin', you always find the positive. Go, talk with the boys. See how they will respond."

"I can tell you one thing: They won't want to leave their dear Mamma! Whatever they choose to do, they will have us in mind too. It won't be easy for any of us. I'll speak with them after supper tomorrow. I need a day to digest everything as we are now. When I speak with them, I want to be calm and ready for their questions and any response."

Monday, we work as usual. When the boys and I return from the fields, we clean up and meet at the dinner table. Antonia had prepared a risotto.

"What's in the rice, Antonia?" I look over at the youngsters and probe further. I raise an eyebrow, asking, "Is that spice a sprinkling of black ants I see? Mixed with some savory viper meat?"

Antonia gives me a stare, shaking her wooden ladle at me. The kids just giggle, hungrily licking their lips. They are accustomed to my joking. I love to hear their laughs fill the air.

While giving me a sideways glance, Antonia dumps a large dollop of rice into my bowl, saying, "This is a special spoonful for the man I love, flavored with tenderized scorpion pincers."

The kids laugh again, but dive into their meals as if they haven't eaten for days.

"Don't worry, kids, the risotto is made with arborio rice, borlotti beans, celery, butter, onion, white wine, olive oil, Parmesan cheese, and some salt, pepper, sage, and garlic. If you don't like it, I'll give you the scorpion rice instead."

A steaming bowl of tender, juicy wild boar meat accompanies the rice dish.

I must compliment the chef and declare, "We are lucky to eat so well every day, but this dinner is something very special. It's not even a holiday! Eat! Eat! Enjoy!"

We then share our stories of the day, except for what Antonia and I discussed about emigration. Elvira helps feed little Carmine. The others wolf down their servings then ask for some extra scoops. I do too, after unbuckling my belt.

I tell the kids they are free to go play but tell the elder boys that we'll go down to the pantano and walk off some of the fine dinner. On the way down we pass friends, give short greetings, but keep a steady stride to the valley. Ahead of us is the vast pantano. The horses and cows are grazing. Hundreds of them. Their colors vibrant under the evening sun. White clouds are turning pink and purple as birds flicker across the mountain ridges. Without work, we are free to absorb the scene. This is our homeland where our great-grandparents lived. Perhaps we're related to the ancient Samnites who once rode Pentro horses across this plain?

"Boys, let's see if this evening we can walk to the far end of the pantano and back. We'll have plenty of time to talk about matters of great importance for you and the whole family. I discussed this earlier with your mom."

I talk with the boys for nearly a half hour on the same topics that Nicola and I had discussed at the cantina. Without alcohol, the matters seem even more pressing. After my discourse comes to an end, there is a short pause. Pasquale is the first to respond.

"Papa, we have thought about this too. Many of our friends have left. They were afraid of the unknown, but most were happy with the choice they made to move. They have good jobs with enough income that they even send money back to their families here."

Michele speaks. "Yes, Papa. If you think it is our best option, we'll give one hundred percent to do well and help the family. But where should we go? How can we prepare?"

"We should continue to discuss this together. When we are all in agreement, we can put our plan into action." I take a deep breath and exhale slowly. "Perhaps it is best if Giuseppe and Pasquale go first. Some fellow villagers have moved to Canada, Argentina, France, or the United States. I think it best to see who we know and contact them for some help. After Giuseppe and Pasquale find jobs and have a place to live, Michele and Carmine can go. Those already there can help you find work and where to rent a room. They can also help you get language instruction. You'll need to get the basics as soon as possible. But don't worry. There are already many Italians in foreign places from all over Italy, mostly southerners. Some have grocery stores and restaurants. This will make the change easier."

Giuseppe and Carmine are eager to leave as soon as possible. They are driven by emotions. They don't even think about preparation. The other boys are more rational.

"OK, Papa," Pasquale says, "I'll gather some information and see how to make the travel arrangements. Probably a ship from Naples to New York, Buenos Aires, or Montreal. I'll work on it and let you know what I learn."

Michele, while looking off at the horses, is in deep thought. He turns to me, looking eye to eye, and asks: "Papa, how about Mamma? Will she, you, and the rest, be OK? I can stay here as long as you want."

I notice that both Pasquale and Michele are tearing up. Their emotions hit me. Attempting to conceal my watering eyes, I turn to look at the sun setting over the mountains. Soon my boys will be gone. None of us can hold back tears and start sobbing.

"It's OK, boys. Keep focused on the future. We'll all be fine. You'll do great overseas. You'll live in a fine home. Your work outside Italy will pay much better than being here. You'll eat well, be among countrymen, making the best of both worlds. And we'll always be in touch. Write often. Remember, you can return here if necessary. But I'm afraid you good-looking boys will probably marry blonde American girls with their long legs and totally forget about us here in Molise!"

"Ah, Papa, we'll be fine," Pasquale assures. "When not thinking of those curvy young fillies, we'll be thinking of you. We know how much work you must do in the field and with the animals, garden, and home."

"No problem. We have Elvira and the other boys to fill your shoes! They are getting older and more helpful each day. Plus, your aunts will help your mom with the daily chores. Even though both of you will be far away, we are family. The distance is not important. Our hearts are close … There is an Italian proverb that may seem insignificant because it is so short and simple. Please remember it: Please remember it: *La famiglia è tutto. Family is everything.*'"

By the time we return home, the sun had set and it's twilight. Antonia is waiting for us, sitting on the long maple bench next to the hearth. One oil lamp is lit. The boys go straight to their room, and I sit next to my love. I tell her about my discussion with the boys and that we will begin to plan for them to emigrate.

Antonia turns sideways to hold my hand. She's pleased with the decision for the boys. She then tells me: "Serafin', I'm pregnant."

chapter 3

The Best Armor Is to Keep Out of Range
la migliore armatura è tenersi fuori portata

"No! There is no benefit in waiting. I leave tomorrow!" So, speaks my twenty-three-year-old, Giuseppe, our eldest. He quickly contacted his best friend in Buenos Aires and immediately started packing. The equally impatient Carmine follows suit. Although they don't even have passports, visas, or tickets, they want to go to Naples tomorrow and get a boat to Argentina as soon as possible. We try to reason with them to no avail. There are no meaningful conversations. No farewell dinner. I'll take them by cart to the train station tomorrow morning. Maybe it is best for the family for them to leave soon. They are fiery stallions that can't be held back.

In contrast, Pasquale and Michele have been steadily preparing to leave for the New World. Three months have passed, and we received letters from a dozen friends. Our best connections are a few distant cousins who live in a large city called Erie in the state called Pennsylvania, facing a vast lake also called Erie. Many from our village have been living there for ten years or more. They say Pasquale can start working upon arrival. All has been prepared for him to leave Italy, except one vital document: his passport with the valid visa, allowing him to go to America.

We have already paid the agent, who was in nearby Isernia city, for the transatlantic ticket from

Naples to New York. Departure date is August 27, 1907, on a steamship called SS *Verona*, built by a Scottish-Irish company for Italian General Navigation. There are 60 first-class and 120 second-class passengers. Pasquale wanted to save money. He'll be one of the 2,500 passengers in steerage. It is the cheapest fare but even that costs almost thirty dollars—about

the immigrants

four months of my salary. We'll pay for Michele's trip soon too. For now, everybody's nervous because it is already August 20 and Pasquale's passport has not been returned yet from the American Consulate General in Naples. They have had the passport for over six months. Knowing the reputation of Italian bureaucracy, we fear that the passport will not arrive in time, or perhaps not at all.

If Pasquale can't leave, we look for something positive. One is that we keep our son close at home. Another is that, for the past year, it seems a relationship has developed between him and Marcella Scalzitti, my friend Nicola's daughter. The Scalzitti family is well respected, and the daughter seems ideal for Pasquale. If fate calls for him to remain in Montenero, then perhaps he can start a nice family here.

The next day I'm with my three eldest sons for the evening milking of our cows. Looking up from squeezing milk into our buckets, we see Giuseppe Colonna entering the barn with a big grin, waving an envelope. He made a special run down to the pantano directly from the post office. Without a word being spoken, we know what he brings.

Pasquale runs, grabbing the envelope and tears it open. "Yes! My passport has the official visa! I'm going to America!"

We must finish milking the cows, but then hurry home with the news. Antonia sees us approaching the door and instinctively knows. Filled with happiness and sorrow, she simply breaks down in tears. The next few days we spend family time together. Relatives and friends visit, including Marcella and her parents. On August 25 we take a wagon to the Montenero train station to see Pasquale off. He'll get to Naples by evening, accompanied by a few other locals who are also making the same trip, stay the night at a hotel, and depart in the morning.

Over the next weeks, there is an uneasy quietness permeating the house. We are all worried about Pasquale's trip, imagining the worst. Was he robbed? Is he seasick? Infected by a contagious disease from other passengers? How will he get from Ellis Island to Erie? During the nights, Antonia and I toss and turn in bed. Finally on September 30 we receive the first letter from Pasquale filled with news.

He arrived at Ellis Island on September 10, and it only took three hours to get through customs. He admits that the worst part was stripping naked to be de-loused. Everyone who traveled in steerage had to be processed this way. He wrote a few paragraphs about what he saw in New York, but two full pages about Erie. He's well cared for, being provided with clothing, a room, and even started work at a big manufacturing company called Continental Rubber Works. The specialty there is making bicycle tires and tubes, but they do make other molded products too. He loves the city, especially the lake—amazed one can't see the land on the other side, which is Canada. He's anticipating the day his brother Michele will arrive.

Almost every month we are getting letters from Pasquale. They are very encouraging for Michele to go to Erie. Until that day comes, we have plenty to do over the cold winter months and during the intense spring planting and fall harvesting.

Our son Berardino was born on a snowy morning February 14, 1910. Fluffy flakes were slowly floating down, blanketing the whole village and surrounding mountains. He brings sunshine even on the most overcast days. But the following year was difficult on us. My sister Giulia died suddenly in the summer at forty-four years old. A cholera epidemic filled the Montenero cemetery to capacity. A hundred people perished. Some crawled to the large pit filled with lime and fell in, dead. The municipal council had already selected an area further from the village for a new cemetery. They began planning it just after the epidemic of 1885 when seventy-two locals died.

Three years have since passed and the village has not recovered. The major news is that our municipal office was just dissolved. This stems from investigations started in 1909. Those at the office work irregularly, the offices are in disorder, and police work is nonexistent. You can imagine how filthy the town is as the animals shit everywhere and nobody cleans the streets. No public lighting. Huge debt with very little income.

Due to the extreme dysfunction of the village, the powers of the royal commissioner were extended on June 5, 1913. Many men and a good number of women have emigrated already, eliminating many of the most capable for office work here. There is no doubt we made the right decision for our sons to emigrate. Eventually, maybe the whole family will go to a place where living would be more civilized. If not to another country, we may consider Rome or Naples.

A big surprise arrives in February, an early birthday present for Michele. We open an envelope from Pasquale. He sent a prepaid transatlantic ticket for his brother! Michele will depart next year on July 20 on a German-built ship, the SS *Moltke*. There is no doubt that Pasquale picked the departure date with Michele's birthday, July 17, in mind.

It seems someone ripped some weeks out of the calendar. A quarter of a year was stolen from us and today is already Michele's birthday. Like a foggy dream, I am witnessing the final days of my son's time here with us. At a farewell gathering, Antonia politely asks the guests, "Would you like another glass of wine?"

"Don't ask, Antonia!" I exclaim. "Just keep pouring!" Bread, cheeses, fruits, and meats are shared abundantly. Seems all our guests are expressing their happiness for Michele by devouring and guzzling what is available. Sharing so brings us joy.

Friends and relatives are toasting Michele,

getting more and more emotional as the evening moves on. My brothers each share a story or give a blessing, especially Pietro, who can't seem to stop jabbering. "Michele is the best nephew! Even without asking, he helps us at home and in the fields. He's as strong as a bull with a heart of a saint!"

The local vino has clearly taken effect. Pietro's eyes are crossing, and his lips are failing to correctly pronounce some vowels and consonants. "We love a you, dear Michelin'! Do well in Americ! We no forget you!"

Oh Lordy, he's making us all start to cry. My perceptive friend Nicola notices this, stands up and starts dancing while singing the Neapolitan folk song "Cicirinella," "She Had, She Had." All joined in for the familiar chorus, "*What did she have? What did she have?*" Nicola sang the verses about the various animals she has, followed by associated vulgar details that made listeners laugh hysterically—Nicola knows how to take everyone's mind to a happy place.

Nicola's daughter, Marcella, hands an envelope to Michele to give to Pasquale. I give him a new pocketknife with an olivewood handle made in the city of Frosolone. It should be useful for his work, at home and in the garden. It's a way for our family to be with him each day. Once he gets to Erie, he'll be able to relax and get settled. He only has one more day here in the village.

The next morning Antonia, Elvira, and I get up at dawn as usual. They immediately make me a coffee and a simple breakfast. I can't eat much after yesterday's feast. The younger siblings continue sleeping, but I see Michele's bed is empty. I guess he's already walking down to the barn in the pantano.

"Gaius, my valiant Pentro steed, this may be the last day I get to visit you, to brush smooth your mane. If I give you a juicy apple, will you let me brush your flank? Of course you will. Here, boy. Enjoy.

"I leave for Naples tomorrow and onward to America to start a new life in a big city. I'll miss the nature here, the fresh mountain air, and seclusion from the rest of the world. But even here, the world is encroaching, so I must leave. It will be good for me and the family.

"Hell, I may even miss cleaning the shit out from your stall! ... Young Filippo will now take my place, under Papa's guidance. He'll learn how to take care of you, clean your hooves and keep you healthy. Like me, you were born and bred in this mountain range. You're a horse with a two-thousand-year history of ancestors in this pantano. Keep your tradition. Keep your independent spirit. Preserve the rare breed. You are special, my dear friend."

Michele doesn't notice that I've entered the

barn. Forehead to forehead, he's holding Gaius with palms around the horse's ears. Wisps of breath float upward from Gaius's nostrils as Michele whispers to him, words only the horse hears.

"Hey, Michele! Good morning! Gaius is looking good. His coat is shiny with the chestnut color. He's happy you've brushed him. I can tell by his smile."

"Thanks, Papa. He's been a good horse over the years. I hope he'll bond with Filippo."

"He certainly will, son," I assure. "Filippo will be here soon. Maybe you can help me milk the cows, then take the rest of the day to keep your mamma company and do whatever else you want. We'll have a nice dinner tonight. I want you to get a good night's sleep."

"OK, Papa. Let's see who can squirt the most milk into these cans!"

The sun swiftly traverses across the mountain ridge. I finish some work in the field and decide to head home a little early to clean up for a dinner with all the family around the table. Luckily my sister-in-law Angela is here to help with baby Bernardino. Elvira is playing *Ice Witch*, a tag game with Filippo and Vincenzo. Michele isn't home yet.

Antonia has prepared Michele's favorite dishes for this evening, the main dish being fusilli pasta with garlic, olive oil, broccoli, and a little salt and red pepper. She has her fresh bread and scamorza that go well with a garden salad. A bowl of juicy pork and sausage that simmered in tomato sauce half the day is brought to the table along with our special homemade wine—a blend of Montepulciano and Sangiovese grapes.

Once seated for dinner, we first say grace,

thanking the Lord for all we have and for the health and safety of our family. We ask for patience and strength to move on in our daily lives, especially for Michele's trip.

The next morning is reminiscent of the day we took Pasquale to the train station six years ago, except Antonia and the siblings will say their farewells at the house. I sit in the carriage holding the horse's reins, watching the hugs and tears flow. I remind them of the time. Michele and his suitcase get in the carriage. Off we go. Family and Montenero now behind us.

Michele gets his ticket from the agent just ten minutes before the train makes its short stop. We hug as if it were the last time we may ever see each other. He will stay the evening in Naples and board the next morning on the SS *Moltke*. He'll be one of the 550 passengers in third class. The ship offers bookings for 390 in first class and 230 in second.

There are only five of us living at home now. Without Michele, it seems half the air has left the room. We heard from other villagers living in Buenos Aires that Giuseppe and Carmine did arrive, after tough passage as stowaways. Giuseppe has since written, although rarely. He assures us that he and Carmine are fine. We've come to not expect much from these boys. Life for them here in Molise has been oppressive. In Buenos Aires, they can focus on themselves. Though it aches our hearts, we wish them well. They know we are always here for them.

Weeks pass and finally a thick envelope arrives postmarked from America. Both sons wrote. Michele provides most of the details. The travel by ocean liner was as predicted. Overall, not bad, even with three days being seasick.

The landing at Ellis Island hit him hard. He was detained by the doctors because of a swollen eye. They thought it might be trachoma, which is highly contagious and can lead to blindness. Some on the ship have been deported because of this. Upon close examination, the docs learned that Michele's puffy eye resulted when he bumped his eyebrow on the ship's guardrail while he was throwing up over the side when seasick.

Being detained gave Michele an opportunity to view areas of Ellis Island that Pasquale didn't see. The medical examination by doctors took only seconds. They quickly scanned each immigrant for sixty symptoms of disease, but they were mostly concerned with trachoma, cholera, scalp and nail fungus, tuberculosis, epilepsy, and mental impairments. It was most sad to see those who were not accepted into the United States. Many individuals, often children, were separated from their families. In the passageway for deportees is a sign with the words: Stairs of Separation.

On the ship manifest, Michele also noticed that for race, he was checked as "Italian South," while those from the north were simply checked as "Italian." This seemed to be a strange distinction for a unified Italy.

Part of Michele's letter reads:

From Ellis Island, I took a small barge to the New York pier. It was made of wood and looked decrepit. It was a short way to the Grand Central Station. When I entered, I had to stop, put my suitcase down, and take in the stunning views. From the outside, the entrance was very impressive.

The interior is just magnificent! The stonework, windows, very high ceilings. I recognize the light, smooth stone used in the walls and archways as travertine. The ceiling vaults are just like in Italy, except here each vault has a glittering chandelier made of bronze. Artworks are everywhere too. Thousands of people are scrambling around. There are over forty platforms. I never knew a train station could be so wonderful. Larger than the pantano! There's much more, but I just don't know how to describe it all.

It took me fifteen hours by train to get to Erie, changing in two cities, Philadelphia and Buffalo. I didn't see much because it was mostly during nighttime. From the train window, I did see miles of lush landscape, farmlands with single homes, and some small cities. I arrived at the Erie station in the afternoon, about three o'clock. As soon as I stepped off the railcar, I see Pasquale waiting with two friends, Pietro and Guido Orlando. The brothers have a Ford Model T car! It cost over 850 US dollars! Close to the city center, there are almost as many cars here as there are horses.

I am staying at the same home where Pasquale is renting, paying 25 US dollars per month. You know that would be my whole month's income in Italy. So strange, but most of the homes here are made of wood! Pasquale said I will get accustomed to it. They are large with much space inside and easy to maintain. There is even running water and electricity. On each floor is a bathroom with a shower and toilet. Pasquale had to show me how to use everything. When I washed up for bed on my first night here, I never felt so clean.

There will be much to do the next few days. Pasquale will give me a tour of some of the city. He said we can walk to the grocery store, shoe repair shop, and clothing stores. Can you imagine, there's a movie theater here too?! We'll visit some factories where I can apply for work. Others from Montenero live in this area. It's hard to believe I am here, in America, thanks to you. I will write again next week.

Love to you and my brothers and sister.
Michele

For the next months, we receive letters every four to six weeks. After six years in Erie, Pasquale has fully adapted. His work is steady, and he even took a citizenship exam and passed! He's an American now. His letters are detailed. He shared the contents of Marcella Scalzitti's letter, the letter she had Michele deliver to him.

She wrote, "At the time when you departed, I learned I was with child. I told my parents that you were the father. They panicked. After a few days, I broke down and told them Eugenio Tornincasa is the real father. I couldn't maintain the lie. You are too good of a man to treat so unfairly. So, nobody in Montenero knows this. All they know is that Eugenio and I got married and I had baby Tonino."

Pasquale was glad an accusation didn't become public. For the past year, he's been regularly dating a Monti girl, named Maria DiFilippo. She's about nine years younger. He doesn't remember her from Montenero. He writes that she is a woman now, and he thinks of her all the time.

Michele started learning English, but it will take

many months before he can take the citizenship exam. There is pressure to study. He wrote:

"I went into a big American grocery store, thinking that it would be easy to buy a few eggs. I didn't know where the eggs were located and tried to ask the cashier *'Dove sono le uova di gallina?'* … but she didn't know Italian. So, I pretended I was a chicken and started to flop my arms and made clucking sounds. Then she knew what I wanted, but it is a very embarrassing way to communicate."

Michele's working two, sometimes three part-time jobs. Just janitorial work, but he is saving some money. He learned that if he saves enough, somehow the bank here will offer a loan to help him start his own business. He became familiar with the bus system, and how the city is laid out on a grid pattern. On special occasions, he and Pasquale visit old friends from the old country who now live in Toronto, Chicago, and Lorain, Ohio.

On weekends, the boys enjoy meeting others at the Montenero Club. Michele writes that it is a fabulous redbrick building with a stone carving high above the entrance with "Vittorio Emmanuel II" inscribed above a lion. On one wall is a painting of the village and the surrounding mountains. To sit here after work, talking with others in the same village dialect, is like being at the old cantina in our hometown. They provide very tasty food too, although Americanized.

Sometimes the boys visit other Italian clubs. There's the Prato Peglina Club on West 16th Street, founded by men from Abruzzo. Many people laugh when it is referred to as the PP Club. Near 15th and Walnut Street, the Nuova Aurora Club is patronized by many Southern Italians, mainly from Calabria and Sicily. They have over 2,200 members. They also visited the Montenero Club on Broadway Street in Lorain, Ohio.

Antonia and I are learning a lot about our boys' lives in Erie. Maybe soon Michele will find better work or start his own business and become a citizen. We pray he will meet the perfect girl to be his wife. He'll certainly treat her well. He deserves a special partner in life.

SEPTEMBER 5, 1914

The postman walks up to the door and knocks. Pasquale opens the door.

"Is Michele DiMarco here? He needs to sign for this letter."

Pasquale calls his brother, "Michele! The postman has brought you something."

Michele runs down from his bedroom and reads to himself:

"TELEGRAM from the Consulate General of Italy, Philadelphia PA. — You are to return to Italy immediately. You have been drafted into the army and must report to the military headquarters in Campobasso before December 1st."

Michele turns white, slumps in a chair and hands the telegram to his brother to read. They look for options, but there is only one. If Michele doesn't return for duty, there could be a huge fine and jail sentence. Even worse, if he doesn't report, he would be marked as a criminal and then he'd never be able to become an American citizen.

chapter 4

Baptism in Reality
il baptismo in realità

At the maritime station in Naples, thousands of people are boarding ocean liners with all the luggage they can carry. Nearly an equal number are arriving from foreign countries. A blue-suited custom officer with a walrus-style mustache greets me: "Michele Antonio DiMarco, your document says you shall report to the military office in Campobasso on December 1st. What do you plan to do until that date?"

"Sir, tomorrow I will take a train to Montenero Val Cocchiara to visit my parents. I'll stay there until I must report in Campobasso."

The officer stamps a page inside my passport: Admitted, October 28, 1913. "Welcome back to Italy, young man. God bless you."

He knows I'll probably be sent off to war soon. I can use all the blessings I can get.

Holding on to the train's carriage doorway while approaching the Montenero station, I lean out to scan the platform. Like a clearing fog around Grand Sasso's peak, Papa comes into view, standing tall with Filippo and Vincenzo on his left side. Mamma is at his right shoulder and Elvira is on her right holding baby Bernardino, who's now a five-year-old. The family appears diminished ... I can only create mental images of my three brothers living overseas.

Papa's face shines with a smile as my mamma and Berardino embrace me. I hear the words "My son. My son," which seem to emerge directly from her heart rather than her lips. The others engulf me. I feel home. I look forward to their surprised faces when I open my suitcase and give them their gifts, including Hershey's chocolate, a rag doll, and a carton of Lucky Strike cigarettes.

The month being here with family will pass quickly. It's euphoric just to return to the former normal ways of life—I bring in wood to put in the fireplace while Mamma is cutting vegetables to make soup. I teach Filippo and Vincenzo how to make slingshots. Elvira complains about me taking up her space. Pappa and I sip some grappa in the late evening.

After Saturday night's dusting of snow across the mountains, the ground sparkles from the golden rays of a November sun. A perfect day to see the pantano from horseback.

"Papa? I'm going to take Gaius for a ride for a few hours. Want to join me? We can be back in time for mass."

"Sure, but I'll have to ask the boss of the house first." Even before he spoke, Mamma was nodding her head, granting permission with a sweet grin.

We walk to the stable in the pantano and saddle up. The horses instinctively know what paths to follow. The vista is stunning in its vastness: A cloudless celestial blue sky offsets the jagged karst ridges on the left, smooth flowing hills to the right, high snow-capped peaks beyond the hills in the foreground to the rear. Ahead, there is the spoon-shaped valley, a wide area that narrows between the flanking hills. Some horses are drinking and grazing along the river while others gallop for no reason except the sheer joy of it. The slow steady current of the Zittola River whispers amid the quiet calm of our ancient valley.

While our horses amble forward, we talk about my time in America, in Erie and its Little Italy amid the clusters of other groups with their strange languages, foods, and habits.

"It's comfortable living there, Papa, but it doesn't ease the pain of not being with the whole family. I talk a lot about this with Pasquale. We know of your sacrifices too. Thoughts of you give us strength. In this chaotic time, we can all benefit from this unnatural separation."

Trying to comfort me, my papa says, "All will be fine, son, especially after you've finished your military service. The French have blocked our military's reach in North Africa but, we have an alliance with Germany and Austria-Hungary that provides some stability. Who really knows what all the politicians and generals are planning! Even without actual fighting, your postings may be difficult at times. I know you'll take extra care. Keep healthy and think of our future!"

His words, "Think of our future," continue echoing in my head.

The few remaining days in the village blur past. Like waking from a dream, I find myself on a train moving toward Campobasso. What stays with me is the sensing of my family's presence, their clothing, the sound of my papa shaving the stubble from his cheeks, the aroma of Mamma's simmering tomato sauce, Berardino's childish giggle. Thoughts like these only bring tears. Arriving at the Campobasso station brings my focus to the present. I'm due to become a soldier.

The military headquarters in Campobasso is bustling with gray-green uniforms. A large part of the processing of conscripts is standing in lines for paperwork, physicals, clothing, and equipment. When these preliminaries are completed, we are ready to go off for training. I get assigned to an infantry regiment. A few days later, on January 9, 1914, I arrive in Modena by train with a few hundred other young men in our dashing new uniforms. The consensus among the recruits is that our new outfits will make us look more attractive to women. I assure you that for some, that would never be enough.

Our weeks of training are easy enough: jogging, crawling, basic hand-to-hand combat techniques— some with the rifle and bayonet—and marksmanship. And taking orders. Orders are screamed at us all the time, even to do simple things. "Make your bed! Button your shirt! Clean the latrine!" Seems we do lots of cleaning, but the duties here are easier than the daily chores I did in Montenero.

During our time off we can relax. I usually go with others to visit Modena and the nearby towns to sample the foods, wines, and look at the women. The females know how to look good in these big cities. I never saw such hairstyles in the village or the snug-fitting dresses. Our village women are more practical, but ... sure is something nice seeing a woman so clean, perfumed, strutting in fine leather shoes. How do their nylons stay up? I guess it's part of living in the big cities here or in other countries.

Generally, the locals are friendly enough to the soldiers in our brigade, but there are times they make fun of our regional dialects or call us hillbillies. Many in our brigade are from central regions. Foods, clothing, dialect, attitudes ... so many differences. Sometimes conflicts occur with the northerners, usually over a woman, gambling, or simply over a bias toward southerners. Results can be entertaining, because the "hillbillies" are tough! So, I've seen a few snobby northerners end up on the floor, bruised and unconscious.

I have made a few good friends. We explore the local areas whenever we have free time. They are from Cerro Al Volturno, Isernia and Campobasso. I tend to be by myself when possible. I like the time to write letters home and to Pasquale. It seems to make time go by faster. Days just never pass fast enough. And then, on June 28, 1914, time took on more urgency with the news that Archduke Franz Ferdinand of Austria was assassinated by a Serbian.

A month later, the Austro-Hungarian government declares war on Serbia. Then comes a speedy string of events: Germany supports the war declaration, France and Great Britain declare war on Germany, Russia supports Serbia, Germany declares war on Belgium and starts an invasion, Austria-Hungary declares war on Russia.

Although Italy's Prime Minister Salandra declared neutrality, the regiments receive notice to immediately prepare for deployment. As an ally, will Italy eventually be called to assist Austria-Hungary's invasion of Serbia? What does our chief of staff, General Cadorna, know that we don't?

For months, we train, clean, and wait. Finally, on May 22, 1915, all the Italian military receive orders for a general mobilization. Where will we be sent? Who will we fight? We wonder how long we'll be kept in the dark about our duties. The next day we learn of a stunning change in our fate: Italy declares war on Austria-Hungary! Our alliance with them and Germany was scrapped after Italy secretly negotiated to ally with Great Britain and France. We're heading to the north-east to fight our former ally.

A great war has begun. The sparks from Austria-Hungary's declaration of war on Serbia ignites hotbeds of aggression in Eastern and Western Europe. Italy is in between. So many countries are involved, I'm not sure of the exact number. It's spreading. Italy has its own front, facing the forces of the Austro-Hungarian Empire, which means we're fighting Germans, Czechs, Pols, Slovaks, Slovenes, Croats, Hungarians, Romanians, and even some ethnic Italians. Years ago, my papa sensed tensions between the nations and predicted this day.

The head of the Italian Army, General Cadorna, is already in the northeast city of Udine making it the headquarters. He's an elderly man of great experience who knows the area well. He has mapped out the front line of roughly four hundred miles, which extends from the southeast Swiss border in the Alps eastward toward the Adriatic. He and the heads of government want to take control of the lands where ethnic Italians live under Austria-Hungarian rule. Cities like Trent, Trst and Gorica should be called Trentino, Trieste, and Gorizia.

Rumor has it that General Cadorna believes that a direct attack eastward through the Isonzo Valley will lead to a quick victory over the Austria-Hungarian forces and open the way to Vienna. Since we have more than double the number of their forces—about

225,000 versus 115,000—those poor bastards will surely run rather than fight.

Two Years and Six Months Later

As prisoners of war, we are herded into a cave with other captured Italians from front-line units. Only two survived from my battalion fighting on the Karst Plateau at the beginning spring of 1916. We captured Mount Sabatino, a main barricade of the Austro-Hungarian's defense of Gorizia, but little else. It was here that a sniper's bullet hit my right shoulder. The enemy employs the tactical rule: "Always shoot at a machine gunner before a rifleman." After being injured, I was unable to lift my weapon. Struggling to find cover, I was hit three times in the legs by machine gun fire. I crawled behind the remains of a tree, a stump left branchless from the morning's artillery barrage.

For twenty minutes I lay there trying to bandage my wounds. An afternoon shadow grew larger as it approached my hideout. I grabbed a short, broken tree branch. As a Slovenian soldier was about to pass the tree stump I was behind, I startled him with my sudden lunge forward. As he started to lift his rifle, I knocked it away to my left with the branch and immediately circled the branch right to strike his kneecap. When he buckled in pain, a blow to the head was his end.

Exhausted, I slumped back to the ground near the stump, then became aware that another Slovenian was charging downhill with his rifle bayonet poised for my stomach. I started to roll away but got cut across my ribs. While rolling, I pulled my knife from its scabbard. As the soldier was about to strike me with the butt of his rifle, my blade caught his stomach first. It's peculiar that my knife blade was made from an old Vetterli-Vitali rifle bayonet.

At dusk a squadron of enemy soldiers was descending Mount Sabatino and spotted me. There was no fight. I didn't resist. They lifted me to my feet, and I limped with them into captivity. Our takeover of Sabatino is necessary for the pursuit of victory in Gorizia. I hope my comrades' sacrifices here will contribute to the goal.

Like many other prisoners here, I'm injured. I'm tending my own wounds: the three bullets in the legs, one in the left shoulder, and a bayonet cut across my left side. I removed the four bullets with my pocket-knife and asked a fellow soldier to cauterize the areas with a red-hot blade. If not done, I knew I would die.

I made a paste from pine resin to cover the wounds. I also saw some wild chamomile, boiled it, then used it to clean and soak the areas. Many plants in this area are different from those around the home mountains in Montenero, so I only use what I recognize to be medically helpful. Over the weeks, I'm healing well, unlike others whose wounds have festered. Each day some die of wounds or malnutrition. I've lost a lot of weight. Not much to eat except grass. Soon, survivors will be transported to various prison camps and probably to the Russian front to do forced labor.

As I heal and wait to be moved out, I try to remember all that I experienced since my first day becoming a soldier in Campobasso. A Slovenian officer confiscated our personal items, including the diary I've kept since the start of the war. I visualize the places I've been and search my memory for the many thoughts and feelings that the war inspired.

When I first arrived up north, the whole area of the battlefront was certainly a foreign land to me. If the presence of war here could be miraculously removed, a grand paradise would emerge. Now, after two and a half years in this area, the land between the Piave and Isonzo Rivers is too familiar. Perhaps all would have been different if General Cardona's plan to get troops to the Isonzo was not delayed by a month due to lack of coordination. That slowdown gave the Austrian-Hungarian troops time to arrive and set up in the most strategic positions.

Our introduction to the Isonzo area was to a turbulent flooding river, which hampered our crossings. When we did cross, we faced enemy defensive trenches, bunkers and miles of barbed wire fencing. Invented in America for cowboys, who knew this razor wire would be used here for a totally different purpose? Month after month, we attacked. We struggled uphill as the enemy shot downward from their machine gun placements. We didn't have enough artillery to weaken their defenses, so Mister Cardona would send wave after wave of our soldiers against the enemy positions to be slaughtered.

We were short on ammunition and weapons. We didn't even have hand grenades. So much of the fighting was just animalistic hand-to-hand combat with knives and fists. My nightmares now consist of images of lifeless corpses who were caught in barbed wire and riddled by machine gun fire. The trenches are putrid with excrement, urine and vomit, while rats scamper around the dead and wounded. When Germany came to the aid of Austria-Hungary, poison gas began to be used, first during the attack on Monte

San Michele. A faint breeze carried the gas over trenches, killing thousands in a few minutes.

We buried the dead behind our lines in shallow graves dug into the hard limestone. Incoming artillery often hits the tombs, blowing corpses' body parts among us. More than two years have passed, and our troops are in the same hellholes.

Our soldiers look ragged and ill. The thunderous roar of the big guns has driven men insane. Morale is low even among the loyal and enthusiastic patriots. For others, as the southerners who feel we're being used as disposable soldiers, the depression is even heavier. Some are suicidal. Some are deserters. Amazingly, there is also a feeling of soldierly brotherhood that brings a nationalistic unity in the face of the enemy.

Our army troops deployed in the north were positioned mainly for defense. The goal there is to prevent the Austrian-Hungarian troops from penetrating further south. They have their own unique problems, including the massive Alps. Soldiers die by bullets and bayonets, but more so from artillery and flying pieces of rock. Some freeze to death. Some get buried alive in avalanches.

To date, perhaps a few hundred thousand soldiers have died on both sides. I'm not sure of the exact number because thousands of new recruits arrive every month. There must be a few million on the front line by now. The Austrian-Hungarians have suffered greatly too. I'm sure they often think of their homes and families as we do. When I was near Gorizia fighting, I finally received an old letter from home that we have a new baby brother, Clemente, born on September 5, 1915, named after our village patron saint.

Thousands of us were transported by train to prisoner-of-war camps in both the Austrian and the Hungarian areas. There are hundreds of locations. Some are very large prison camps with forty thousand to one hundred thousand inmates. There are also stations for quarantine, punishment, simple confinement, and work camps.

Most captives live under harsh conditions in the war camps. Great numbers are dying of battle wounds, but are also wasting away from lack of food, bitter cold, accidents, and diseases like tuberculosis. The Italian government was asked to provide supplies but refused to send any aid. We learned that they labeled us POWs as deserters, undeserving of food parcels. Perhaps the true reason was that rations were needed in Italy.

In a way, it seems us southern "hillbilly" prisoners are lucky because many of us are being sent to farming areas to work. Both Germany and Austria-Hungary find it impossible to bear the expense of supporting the tens of thousands of Allied prisoners in camps. Their farmers and others were mobilized, taken away from this vital work. We are filling in, helping feed our captive Allied brothers and our enemies in the Austria-Hungarian Empire.

From open railway cars, we see a few camps on the way to Ljubljana, Slovenia. From there we move on, closer to the Carpathian Mountains. We change lines and end up in an extensive agricultural area in Hungary called Kenyérmezo (Bread Field). Probably because of my experience with horses, I get assigned basic duties tending to horses and tilling the soil. The Austria-Hungarians have over one hundred thousand horses in military service. Our work helps provide healthy horses and a food supply to their military and civilians. We are valuable for this slave work, so we eat and sleep relatively well. Hell, unlike those in the large prison camps, we are even given new underwear!

Over the weeks we get new arrivals from the front, prisoners put to work on the farm. We look forward to any news they can give. In the first week of August 1916, fighting commenced again and our troops gloriously captured Gorizia! A major victory for Italy! The cost? More than six thousand Italian soldiers died, with over thirty thousand wounded.

A fortuitous opportunity comes on August 20, 1916, Hungary's most important national holiday. It celebrates Saint Stephen, who became the first king of Hungary a thousand years ago. As we prepare to retire to our bunks for the night, there is a change of guard. The night guard has obviously heavily imbibed a liter or two of strong fruit brandy. Shortly after taking his chair next to the doorway, he passes out in a deep slumber! Regardless of outcome, I decide to escape. If caught, I could be executed for trying. I had thought about this for the past month and felt I could get a good distance away without being noticed.

As the guard raucously snores, I quietly dress under my blanket then place some clothing and a pillow under the covering, trying to make it appear as if I am sleeping in the bed. I have a backpack with a few days' supply of food and a canteen of water. Most of the prisoners who are still awake keep silent. A few whisper, "Good luck." Rather than try to bypass the guard and go out the door, I stealthily slip out a window at the back of the room.

chapter 5

Out of the Pan, Into the Fire
dalla padella, nel fuoco

Here on the Kenyérmezo farm, I know the horses better than I do the people. I don't remember the guards' names. I've named about fifty of the two hundred horses in the pasture. One mare reminds me of Gaius that, upon first sight, I named *Numen*—after the Samnite belief in divine will. As I approach the horses, they recognize my scent and don't make a sound. I calmly saddle Numen and mount. We move off southward in a slow walk for the first mile on a dirt road. Then, into an abyss of darkness, we head through miles of open countryside at half gallop.

Wanting to get as far away from the farm as possible, I ride until sunrise. It seems I've gone about twenty-five miles. At a small village crossing is a road sign saying Budapest is just fifteen miles to the east. I tie Numen to a tree near a stream in a little gully where she can eat some grass and drink. I gather an armful of hay from the fields to give her too. It's a perfect spot to rest, just out of vision of anyone in the nearby village. As soon as I lie down on the riverbank, I quickly drift into dreamless sleep.

A few hours later, I awake to some noise from the village as the local peasants begin their day's work. My mind turns to the goal of getting out of Hungary. Anyone here can potentially turn me into military authorities. I'd be shot as an escapee. Romania is a neutral country, so I feel pressed to get there as soon as possible. Not wanting to draw attention from the locals, I continue southward at a slow pace. At dusk, Numen alternates between a gallop and a half gallop. During the next two days I keep the pace, only sleeping about four hours per night.

On the fourth day just before dusk, we cross into Romania at a border village called Nădlac. Feeling safe from enemies, my whole being relaxes for the first time since being drafted! It seems there may be a population here of three or four thousand people. They probably speak Romanian and some Hungarian. If I meet any friendly persons who would be sympathetic to an escaped Italian prisoner, they may be able to provide some helpful information as well as some food. I decide to take a risk to seek help. Figuring a caring priest would be my best option, I see a church bell tower and ride to the front door of the house of prayer. A sign says it's Saint Nicholas Church. This seems auspicious since we also have a Saint Nicholas church in Montenero.

The church is empty of people. It's quiet with a hint of incense in the air. I kneel in a pew, bow my head, and thank God for getting me to this sacred place. My list of things to be thankful for is long and my thoughts flow on endlessly. A wooden door to the rectory slowly creaks open and a priest is surprised to see me bowing at the feet of crucified Jesus. He walks toward me smiling and speaks a few sentences I can't understand. I rise and smile too, mainly because he looks childishly cherub-like, despite the fact his cropped silvery hair shows otherwise.

"Padre, I am Italian. I am soldier." I point north and then to my feet, and say, "I come from Hungary. I want to go to Italy."

The priest's eyebrows rise as he nods his head. He speaks again. Within his sentences I understand some words: "soldier," "Hungarians," "war." He signals for me to follow him into the rectory. He gestures for me to sit at the kitchen table and immediately puts some bread, cheese, and fruit in front of me. He starts making some coffee and goes out the back door. Two minutes later he returns with a neighbor who speaks some Italian. Soon, they know my story.

Father Silviu invites me to stay in an extra room usually used for acolytes. Grigel, his translator friend, will stay too. As Grigel stables my horse, the priest shows me where I can wash. He sets out some towels and some fresh clothing. Such kindness is shocking after what I've experienced these past few years. Father Silviu exhibits God's grace through his human actions.

I stay with the priest for three more days. It's been weeks since I escaped. Today, August 27, news spreads through the village: Romania has joined the Allies in the war's fight against the Central Powers—Germany, Austria-Hungary, the Ottoman Empire, and Bulgaria. Without my knowing, Father Silviu and Grigel are planning how to get me through Bulgaria, an enemy territory, to neutral Greece. Once in Greece, I could get a boat to Italy. From this village of Nădlac, it's about 480 miles to the Greek border.

Their plan? Grigel has a connection who can make a fake Romanian passport for me. We will use my photo from my POW identification card. They will include a document in Romanian that states that I will go to Thessaloniki, Greece, to study theology at Aristotle University. Official church stamps in red will make it look authentic. I should shave my head and dress for the role, including a necklace with a small cross worn outside the shirt. The document will state that I'm a deaf mute. I can take a train from the nearby city of Arad to Thessaloniki. This is a plausible scenario, but not foolproof. I agree to do it. I ask Grigel to take Numen. At first, he refuses to accept such a valuable animal, but realizes I can't take the horse on the train anyway. He leaves the house for twenty minutes and returns to give me enough cash to cover my whole trip back to Italy.

My new friends have done much to prepare for my trip. I can never repay them. I feel clean, rested and well-fed. It takes fourteen hours to reach the Bulgarian border without any incidents. It will take sixteen more hours to reach Thessaloniki. This stretch of the trip is nerve-racking. Bulgarian soldiers are either going to or coming from Serbia, occupying the eastern half of the country while Austria-Hungarian troops occupy the western half. Surprisingly, I'm basically ignored during the trip. To onlookers, I'm just a religious deaf mute, as harmless as a fly. Another flush of inner peace comes when entering Greece. Now, Italy doesn't seem so far off.

Arriving at the Thessaloniki station at 9 a.m., I find a hotel, take a shower, shave, and nap for a few hours. When I awake, I realize I haven't eaten for two days. The hotel exchanges some of my Romanian leu for Greek drachmas. The Aegean Breadbasket Restaurant is on the hotel's first floor. I see a table near a window facing the street and sit.

A young waitress gracefully walks toward me with a menu in hand. In my eyes, she appears as Aphrodite, the Greek goddess of love and beauty. Her pure ink-black hair cascades down her back, shimmering in the light shining through the window. Her hazel brown eyes, set under long lashes, contrast with her fair alabaster skin. The pastel yellow restaurant uniform wraps her from neck to knees, unable to conceal her ideal classical proportions. Handing me the menu, she says something. I find myself mesmerized by her mouth as her velvety lips enunciate syllables I can't understand. She pauses waiting for me to reply and I start stuttering like a machine gun.

Embarrassed and thinking how ridiculous I must appear, I can't help but break out in laughter. I'm laughing so hard at myself that she starts laughing uncontrollably too. I apologize, forgetting I'm speaking in Italian.

"Signorina, sorry I am so childish in your presence. Please forgive me."

Her stunned face expresses the realization that I don't speak Greek. Then she speaks in Italian: "Excuse me. My Italian not so good. I learn some from my brother's wife. She from Messina. Ship company worker."

We exchange some details, and she learns about my escape from the Austrian-Hungarians. Her name is Evangelina Panos. She mentions that, because of the fighting in the Balkans, the Greeks are anxious that they may be drawn into the conflicts too.

"Maybe we can talk later, after my work?"

I'm taken off guard, but *yes* comes out of my mouth instantly.

My priority for the day was just to have dinner, but now I look forward to the evening. First, I must eat. I can't read the menu and I'm not sure what to order. So, Evangelina offers "to bring something good." Ten minutes later comes a tray with a fine vegetable stew and small side dishes of cheese, bread, a salad, and red wine. Food for a king.

When I pay for my meal, Evangelina says, "Meet me front of hotel six o'clock and we go walking to the waterfront. OK?"

"Perfect. See you then." I think to myself how this kind of meeting wouldn't happen in Montenero. I feel I'm the one in a million struck by a lightning bolt. After the previous years in war zones, this new relationship, with a real woman, is a challenge. I'm not sure how to act or what to say. I'll need to go on pure instinct.

Before going to my room, I head to the front desk and pick up a postcard that has a colorized photo of the hotel on the front. I write a note:

Father Silviu, Grigel, and Numen,
Arrived here today thanks to your guidance.
God bless you!
Your friend forever, MD
Addressed to: Saint Nicholas Church
                Nădlac, Romania

The clerk at the desk says he will mail it for me.

I go to my room and rest for a few hours. At 5:30 I wash up with cold water to revive myself and dress. I leave the room ten minutes early to meet Evangelina in front of the hotel. She's already there, hair blowing in a soft breeze, looking fresh and happy.

"Hello, Michele! You have only seen the train station and the hotel. This evening, I take you to the port. You can see the Aegean Sea for the first time."

"That sounds wonderful! I have never visited

Greece before. All I know is from some books and stories from others in Italy."

"Well," she adds, "much has changed here. Just four years ago, during the Balkan War, the Greek Army took this city from the Ottoman Empire. It is much quieter now and we are recovering."

As we walk toward the port, I can hear people speaking different languages. Evangelina says that after five centuries under Turkish rule, their language is the second most common here. Ladino is most common, being the special blend of Judeo-Spanish. The largest group living in Thessaloniki are Jewish. The Greek population is third.

A slow fifteen-minute walk and we get to the seaside. One area of the port is filled with cargo ships from many countries. The White Tower stands out in the distance. It was once a fortress and later used as a prison.

I turn to Evangelina after observing the structure. "It is not so white, but a natural stone color."

"Yes, you're right. It got the name back in 1890. A convict whitewashed the whole building himself, earning his freedom. Today it is a museum and the symbol of the city."

She gets excited and offers a way for me to stay longer in Thessaloniki. "Hey, Michele, we are not far from the Aristotle University. Perhaps you would like to go there to study and become a priest?"

I take a quick up-and-down look at her physique, then roll my eyes. Smiling, I ironically affirm that "My only goal in life is to become a monk." She thinks a moment, translating in her head, then her eyes sparkle with satisfaction, knowing she's captured my attention.

Evangelina is as smart as she is good-looking. With a sense of humor too. It is a special evening walking along the bay's treelined front. We stroll through the Ladadika District, where there are many cozy restaurants along the cobblestone streets. For a long time, it has been the central market where people gather. From here, it takes a few minutes to Aristotle's Square.

Evening turns to night as the streetlights illuminate our steps. We head toward Evangelina's apartment close to the hotel. She moved here four years ago just before the Balkan Wars broke out. Her family, like mine, lives in a small village about ninety miles away. They are farmers mainly growing olives. She came here to go to college, but the war changed everything, including her plans.

"Can you stay longer, Michele? Some more days? You are different than the Greek men. You listen. You care about each minute. You feel for your family and others. You're polite. You treat me with respect. It is nice to spend this time together. I don't have to work the next two days."

Logic tells me what I should do. "Evangelina, I should get to Italy soon to let the military, and my parents know I'm alive. You understand?" But the emotions are overwhelming. "I am lucky to be alive, to be here, to meet you ... OK. I'll stay a few more days."

Hearing my answer, the young lady accompanying me all evening so reservedly, spontaneously jumps forward, hugging me tightly. I freeze for a few seconds, and she starts to let go. Then I respond, pulling her close, and her grip tightens too.

The next two days are enchanting. We visit

ancient Roman and Byzantine sights, including the Church of Saint Demetrius and the Roman Arch of Galerius. Time stops at a café, simply sitting together enjoying the atmosphere and glasses of cold Fix Hellas beer.

Most enjoyable is my last day here. Evangelina introduces me to her brother Kostas and his wife, Gloria. The sister-in-law makes a fine Sicilian-style dinner at their home. They are more fluent in Italian than Evangelina and conversation is easy with them. A delightful couple with welcoming hearts. We spend almost the whole day together. Knowing I will depart in the morning makes this most enjoyable day also the saddest.

When we get to Evangelina's apartment it's almost midnight. My train time is 6:10 the next morning. She starts work at 7:00. It seems impossible to say goodbye to each other. In front of her door, we embrace and are overcome with passion. The door seems to open by itself, and she draws me in. The next four hours are filled with an intimacy I've never experienced before. By her timidness and nervous shivering, it is clearly her first time giving herself so fully to anyone. We are both surprised, but it also seems natural. Is it the warring years that make us dare to fall in love only knowing each other such a short time? Or is it as a philosopher said: "The soul does not keep time. It merely records growth."

At 5:30, I must run to the station. I dress quickly, then stop to gaze at Evangelina in bed. She's propped up, disheveled coal black hair against a pillow, covered to her shoulders in a white sheet, arms crossed with hands over her breasts. Her doe-like eyes express a silent sorrow at my imminent departure. Standing at the foot of the bed, I pull the sheet slowly down, exposing her body inch by inch. She's a goddess in body and mind. Perhaps I'm crazy to leave my Aphrodite. I brush kisses upon her from feet up to her velvety lips that I will never forget.

The next three days I travel by train, bus, and boat. The ship from the Greek port of Igoumenitsa to Bari takes twelve hours. Although the distance from Bari to Campobasso is not so far, the train and bus connections make the trip another full day. When I finally arrive in Campobasso, I find the military headquarters is very busy processing new recruits and records of actions on the front line. I'm added to the roster on September 5, 1916, assigned to the 14th

Infantry Regiment, which means I'll be heading back to the Isonzo. I have one week to visit family in Montenero.

For many months, it was impossible to exchange letters with my family. Nobody knew my whereabouts or of my capture. Villagers do know that thousands of souls were lost on the front line, so most presume the worst for me. But I arrive at the Montenero train station before noon and walk an hour to get to the village. "Who's that approaching?" Those in Montenero are shocked seeing me walking down Via Castellana toward my parents' home. They wonder if it is a ghostly apparition or Michele in the flesh. My mamma hugs me at the doorway, crying uncontrollably. Baby Clemente is just over a year old and is understandably apprehensive at my approach. I see my parents and am saddened that they have aged quickly over the past few stressful years. Sons have departed. My papa's mother, Concordia, died on August 3, while I was laboring on the farm in Hungary.

Pasquale has been thoughtful. He's been sending money and some clothing whenever he can. No news from the brothers in Argentina for many months, so we also fear something bad has happened there. I talk with my papa and try to get caught up with as many details as possible. He learns of my time on the front, my wounds, prison camps, and escape. He looks at my scars and we agree that I not let my mamma or the kids see them at this time.

Elvira is a responsible adult now at twenty years old. She's engaged to Filippo Iacobozzi. They are planning to marry and eventually emigrate to Chicago. The two other teenage brothers are doing well and work hard for the family. They are mastering work in the fields and with the animals. But I notice areas where I can make life easier for my parents. For a week, I do what I can to help make daily living more comfortable at home and in the barn. But all too soon I must leave again to look the enemy in the face.

Travelling in Italy is chaotic. New recruits along with military and food supplies are on their way north. Thousands of wounded soldiers are being transported south from the front. Many are amputees. When I arrive in Udine, the war front is very familiar to me, except now there are many more soldiers than a few years ago. Troops are at rest following a successful battle on the Karst Plateau.

As October begins, so does the next battle. I'm back on the line again with a new machine gun in hand. Our goal is to extend our reach around Gorizia. The attack begins with our tremendous artillery power showering bombs on the enemy followed by our advancing foot soldiers. Fighting only lasts for three days, from the 10th to the 12th, without any result except for over 50,000 casualties on our side. Nobody is sure of the exact numbers killed because there are many missing or captured.

In November, we attack again across the Karst Plateau. As in previous years, I see the Austrian-Hungarian troops have the positional advantage on the high terrain. They have fewer battalions and artillery than we do but remain formidable. General Cardona halts the attack on November 4, and we resign to regroup for the coming year.

November and December pass and we find ourselves bored waiting for the next four months without activity on the front. Seems the military leaders are deciding how to coordinate action on the Western Front and the Italian Front. Germany has sent more troops and supplies to assist the Austrio-Hungarians.

As we wait for the start of the next battle, many soldiers go on leave. They usually head into the nearby towns to drink and look for women. The looser the woman, the better. They always return with colorful stories—no doubt exaggerated—of their exploits with the *smanfaraccia*, the town streetwalkers. I think about joining the men on their lecherous excursions, but Evangelina comes to mind. I can't. I would feel unfaithful to my future wife, even if she is not Evangelina.

The combative goal now has widened from a focus around Gorizia to a twenty-five-mile line across the Karst Plateau with hopes to get to Trieste and to Mount Škabrijel facilitating the way toward the Slovenian capital. For two days, May 10–12, 1917, our heavy artillery pounds the enemy. They counter with their own artillery and troops. We manage to get close to Trieste but fall short by fifteen miles. The Austrian-Hungarian counter movements force us to retreat, and we lose all that we've gained over the past two weeks of fighting. We sustain many casualties, including 36,000 dead Italian soldiers. Half of that number for the enemy.

By mid-August, Cardona is ready to go again. This time with more artillery and more men. We fire over five and a half million artillery shells. As in the previous battle, there is some success. Both sides eventually become exhausted, and the battle comes to a standstill on September 12. Another 30,000 dead on our side with over 100,000 wounded. The enemy's number of casualties is half ours.

In mid-October, Italian reconnaissance aircraft notice a large German force arriving to bolster the Austrian-Hungarian line. We didn't know of their plan to use poison gas to the fullest extent possible. German military officers are utilizing scientists and chemists as advisors. In late October their offensive begins, focusing on the area around Caporetto. Cannisters are fired, blanketing the Italian trenches. Hundreds die, while others flee. The gas masks used by Italian troops are only useful for up to two hours. Bombardment follows and enemy troops flush forward well supplied with flamethrowers, mortars, hand grenades, and new German model light machine guns.

Italian troops must retreat over two hundred miles all the way to the Piave River. This is certainly Italy's greatest defeat in the war so far. More than 13,000 soldiers are killed, 30,000 wounded and almost 275,000 are taken prisoner. A great amount of equipment is lost to the enemy too, including over 3,000 artillery pieces. Mister Cardona is forced to resign. Armando Diaz is his replacement as chief of staff. As a result of this disaster, now known as the Battle of Caporetto, some support will eventually arrive from the French and the British. Thus, on November 19, 1917, after two and a half years, ends the sting of battles along the Isonzo. The Piave River becomes our new line of defense.

Our army now takes strategic positions of advantage on the higher ground, mainly around Mount Grappa. Mid-November through the end of 1917, Austrian-Hungarian troops attack but fail to gain ground. During late June the following year, a second attack along the Piave ends in yet another failure for the enemy. Their goal of reaching Venice will not materialize. Under General Diaz's reasonable direction and strategic mobility, our troops stabilize the area.

After two battles on the Piave River, the Austrian-Hungarian forces are beginning to show signs of weakness. It is the perfect time for Italy to launch a massive counteroffensive. The main line of attack is directed toward the city of Vittorio Veneto. Italian, French, and British divisions begin a forward press on the night of October 23 with a full attack the next day. In just over a week, the Italian artillery fires more than 2,400,000 shells. An infantry group from the United States also joins in the offensive.

As the enemy troops are pushed out of Vittorio Veneto, it becomes evident that their military power is collapsing. And, according to the rumors, the adhesiveness of their political power is likewise cracking. In October, some countries under the Austria-Hungarian Empire are declaring independence. A few ethnic groups are breaking away and start planning to form new countries. Seeking to control their own destiny, Hungary breaks its ties with Austria. As a result of the political crumble, our enemies haphazardly retreat from the battlefront. In pursuit, our troops advance quickly to the east. We have an amphibious force take over Trieste. On November 3, Austrian officials face their desperate situation and cease hostilities.

The humbled Austro-Hungarians and the Germans request a truce. Demands are made on them to evacuate the lands occupied since mid-1914, plus much of the nearby territories. Italy obtains possession of not only the areas where ethnic Italians lived in the Isonzo Valley, Gorizia, and Trieste, but also comes to occupy lands west of Switzerland, north of Udine and Trieste, and lands south of Trieste along the Adriatic coast.

When I first arrived on the frontline battlefield in the spring of 1915, we had a force of 300,000 soldiers. At the end of the war on November 3, 1918, we numbered nearly five million. We have finally taken control of the lands that our government long desired. At war's end, about half a million Italian soldiers had died on the front with nearly a million wounded. A tremendous cost to our military as well as the toll on our civilians throughout the country.

I am alive. I'll soon be on my way back home, excited to see the family, the home village, and the Pentro horses galloping across the valley's sublime expanse. Thoughts of Pasquale doing well in America pleases me, although he lives a world away. And, even after two years on the violent war front, images and memories of Evangelina still regularly visit my mind. Soon I'll be on a homebound train as a free man, untied to military duty. Chains in my heart are pulling in different directions. In Montenero, I'll either decide on my future path, or see where fate takes me.

chapter 6

Eat the Soup or Jump Out the Window
mangiar questa minestra o saltar questa finestra

November 3, 1918, is a happy day for millions of soldiers as it signifies the end of the war. It will take many more months just to clean up the aftermath, both on the front and behind the lines: care for the wounded, repair and transfer of equipment, helping the displaced citizens, improving the infrastructure such as bridges, and much more. We're thrilled that there is no need to carry our weapons any longer, not so thrilled at some of the backbreaking labor we are assigned to over the next months.

It is a pleasure to see the scars of war-torn areas heal and return to normal life. After six months, the people in many villages and cities feel hope for the future. They are inspired to work hard, planting crops and tending their animals. Many of the young are going to schools. Letters from home say even in the poorer southern regions, farms are becoming productive and there is bread on the table. Even with the progress, it is nonetheless a very difficult time.

For me, the real day of freedom comes on September 8, 1919, when I am placed on unlimited leave. My military service ceases. I'm discharged. I'm liberated. I'm emancipated! I pack what little belongings I have into a new Alpini mountain rucksack that I recently won in a card game. The next day a military truck takes fifty of us to the railroad station in Treviso, which gets us by train to Venice. From there, our group splits, departing to various destinations. My connection takes me to Bologna, changing in Pescara for Sulmona, changing again then onward to Montenero's station. To make the connections, I have some overnight stays.

In Sulmona, I buy a large bag of confetti candy made with the Jordan almonds that the whole family can enjoy. I should be in Montenero on September 14, three days before my mamma's birthday. I want to get her something special. When I walk into a store on this chilly fall day, I see a beautiful wool blanket made in Taranta Peligna and purchase it on the spot. This beautiful bedcover will keep my parents warm through the winter and the floral design will brighten their room.

At 12:10 in the afternoon, my train arrives at the Montenero station. The rich blue skies are accented by a few feathery white clouds and familiar mountainscape. The air is crisp, making the hour stroll to the village very comfortable. If my recent letter arrived, my family should know I'll be arriving, although they wouldn't know the exact time or day.

I approach and stop in front of the house, gazing at the history the edifice presents to my eyes. After four years and nine months in the army, the old home now tells me its story. With vibrant images in mind of my young papa and grandfather, I can feel the muscle strain of their work remodeling our three-hundred-year-old home of solid heavy stone. Layers of years pile up, recording my mamma's kneading dough, knitting sweaters on the balcony, cutting vegetables, and stewing meats to feed the family. Like it was yesterday, I picture my barefoot siblings running in and out of the house, chasing a pig or chicken for fun, and tormenting each other with practical jokes. My mamma would bandage a bruised knee if I fell and comfort me until the tearing stopped. She turns fifty-four in a few days. My papa regularly lifted my spirits with his steadfast encouragement. I always wish I had his strength and practical wisdom.

The front door is closed to keep the heat in. I yell loud enough to penetrate the door: "Hey, you inside! Is this the house where live the best parents in the world?!"

My mamma is the first to run out, powdery flour on her baking apron and cheeks. She hugs me like one of the local Marsican brown bears. Dad comes out with his beaming smile, tightly squeezing both my mamma and me, then he picks my backpack off the ground. Berardino is peeking from the doorway trying to figure out who I am. When he does, he joins us in sharing hugs too. We enter the house, and I see four-year-old Clemente with no care in the world taking an afternoon nap in his crib.

I settle in the house, wash, and change out of my uniform into comfortable civilian clothes. Oh, what a nice feeling! I know it's not, but our home interior seems designed for royalty. Years in trenches gives one a different perspective and sense of values. Being at home makes me feel like I am almost a normal person.

Mom is speedily creating one of her amazing meals. I think she works by instinct and magically produces the most succulent meat dishes, zesty sauces, and accentuates the most natural vegetable flavors with her choice use of oil and spices.

While I'm changing clothes, she berates me.

"Michele! You look like a skinny spaghett'! You're so thin, I'm surprised your pants don't fall down. Don't you worry. We'll get some weight on you. Soon you'll be as rotund as Father Santucci. He barely fits into his cassock now."

Near dinnertime, Papa returns from the stable with Filippo, and Elvia returns from visiting her future mother-in-law, Luigina Iacobozzi. Vincenzo is not present, so I ask if he will join us. Mamma is facing the stove with her head down. Dad silently motions for me to join him outside. He says we have much to talk about since we could not regularly communicate for the past few years. We sit on a stone wall near the house, and he begins by telling me about my brother Vincenzo.

"Just after you left in September 1916, your brother got drafted that November. He just turned fifteen years old. He went for military training up in Modena."

Dad's eyes water up, and my mind jumps to a conclusion: "Dad, did he get killed in the war?"

After a long pause, he inhales slowly and deeply, then says, "No, my son. For me, it is worse. On January 17, 1917, he died from stab wounds following an argument with some soldiers from Turin. He never made it to the front line. The police report said he was beaten for homosexual activity with a local man, but we have never had any indication he had that tendency, so I can't believe their report. I don't know of any reason for such brutality. The military shipped his body here. He's buried in the new cemetery. We will go visit him soon."

My heart bleeds. We hug each other in silence, no doubt thinking of this loss and of the void of any news from my brothers in Argentina.

"And there is one more story to tell you now, since you will no doubt hear about it from everyone in the village. I was arrested ..."

Before he could explain any further, I exclaim, "What? What possibly could you do that would be an offense!?"

"Not just me, son, but one hundred and twenty-two others as well! Three years after you were born, the government made a special study on the pantano. They discovered that the marsh had a layer of peat several meters thick that totals over two hundred and fifty million tons! So of course, this news brought get-rich-quick schemes from developers. Near the end of the Great War, there was a shortage of coal. Some wanted to turn the pantano into a hydroelectric basin while others wanted to sell the peat as fuel. The village administrators were seriously considering selling it.

"While you were fighting on the Karst Plateau in the summer of 1917, villagers attacked members of the municipal council causing some injuries. Your Uncle Pietro and eight others were behind bars for six months before being freed and pardoned. The pantano has been our means of living for a thousand years and now greedy developers wanted to take it from us. The intensity of the problem has kept on the minds of everyone here."

I interject some questions. "So, since then, the pantano was left as is? The farming and work there continue?"

"Son, that was just the beginning. In January of 1918, during the festival of Saint Antonio, all hell broke loose. Pent-up anger burst into a violent attack directed toward the town hall, where police stood guard with rifles affixed with bayonets. From the archway above the New Gate, women hurled stones and vulgarities toward the town hall doors. Police fired their guns to try to scare off the crowd. Sixty-six-year-old Francesca Di Marco, wife of Antonio Scalzitti, was stabbed in the stomach by a bayonet and died.

"The next day, soldiers arrived from Sulmona and camped in the square. They were sent here because some officials thought the revolt in Montenero was political. Because the protests were over the topic of peat, the soldiers generally remained passive. However, the police became active, trying to arrest those involved in what we call the Peat Rebellion. Unfortunately, a Scalzitti boy, who was only eleven years old, was struck on the head and died. Some escaped. In the end, one hundred and twenty-three people were arrested, forced into a large truck in front of the Palazzo De Arcangelis and jailed in the district prison in Forlì del Sannio. Most spent a month incarcerated, but others were jailed for six months. I was one in that group. Uncle Pietro and his son too.

"Four police were questioned about the killing of the Scalzitti woman and the child, but it could not be proven what son of a bitch was responsible. In all, one hundred and fifteen villagers were accused of crimes of violence and threat against the royal police. About forty were detained in Isernia. Others were accused of complicity in crime or personal injury to the royal police. Your Uncle Pietro unsuccessfully attacked a brigadier with a weapon. About a month later, more than one hundred detainees were released. The remaining nine were held for about six months. Many cases are still not closed. We're waiting with hopes that all will eventually be pardoned."

"Jesus Christ! Papa, you were fighting a battle here while I was fighting on the front line!"

"Yes, son. You will hear many stories about the Peat Rebellion. It affected everyone here."

My papa smiles and says, "I hope you don't mind that you are associated with a criminal like me for a father. And now there's talk about building a brewery near the station, *Beer of Abruzzo*, using the water from the Sangro River and the peat from the pantano for fuel."

I laugh and give my full support for his taking part in the rebellion. "Papa, I'm proud of you. You are a soldier too, standing up for what is right and good for all the people. The businesspeople all too often take advantage of the hardworking farmers here."

My papa rises from the stone wall. "Let's get back in the house. Dinner must be ready by now. We don't need to talk about any serious matters in front of the family. They all know what has happened and words don't make the loss of Vincenzo any easier."

Our family members gather around the table. Like days in the distant past, Papa jokes, Mamma serves, and we all tell stories of our day. We are with each other, through thick and thin. Each day we work hard as usual. We live in accord with the seasons. If we're lucky the crops will be abundant, and our cows will produce fine milk. This is our farming life here in the village. We've lived in harmony with the land. It is the political seasons that prove difficult. There is still much talk in the family and within the village about emigration.

My parents believe I should return to America. Pasquale is in Erie and there is much opportunity.

He's married and they just had a baby girl on May 5 they named Antoinette. I am familiar with Erie and know I could easily settle there. Sure, it would be good for Pasquale and me, and we can best support our parents and siblings from there. Like waking from a dream, I must forget about Evangelina. We could not communicate while I was on the war front. Much time has passed. She's probably married by now. Reality has set in, giving me direction. It becomes clear that I should prepare to return to America. I can plan to leave after the summer harvest, but I am in no hurry.

Our focus turns to the Christmas holiday season. We celebrate Saint Nicholas on December 6 as protector of children. Berardino is happy to receive a gift, but it is little Clemente who gets showered with toys and affection. My mamma is cooking and baking nonstop with friends and relatives visiting. We visit our closest relatives and friends too.

This holiday seems to blend with the Epiphany on January 6. At first, Clemente panics and begins crying when he sees the friendly witch La Befana—a local lady in a costume—show up on the street. When she puts some candies in his shoes, he suddenly is full of chuckles.

As we reach the mid-year of 1920, I mail my passport to the United States Consulate in Naples to apply for a visa. With some luck, I may receive it in three or four months. After it arrives, I'll book the steamer and write Pasquale my arrival date to New York. He's already preparing where I can stay and talking with potential employers. In his recent letter, he informs us that on September 6 they had a stillborn child. They named him after my papa. If they have another boy, his name will be Serafino. I think about this but try to keep my mind here in Montenero savoring my moments here with family.

Whenever walking around the meandering pathways in Montenero, the past always blends into the present. In the main square, a newly carved marble plaque was set on the outer wall of the municipal building to honor the fallen soldiers from the Great War. It reads:

Citizens
Proudly Hold
in Permanent Memory
Montenero V. September 6, 1919

This plaque was created from the most
holy devotion and perpetual belief in the
just conquest of the natural borders of
our homeland and for the freedom of our
ethnic brothers, with the effort of these
fallen Italian heroes who courageously
fought in this war of national redemption.

• Marcello Bonaminio	• Biase Cacchione
• Alfonso DiFiore	• Isidoro DiFilippo
• Erminio Del Sangro	• Giovanni Micigan
• Achille DiNicola	• Cosmo DiLuca
• Alessandro Fioritti	• Gregorio DiNicola
• Romeo Procario	• Giulio Freda
• Nicola Mannarelli	• Giuseppe Procario
• Emidio Orlando	• Giulio Gigliotti

The plaque was carved with the support of the villagers to "proudly hold in permanent memory" fourteen local men. This list also includes two men born here, but who lived in the United States and fought with the United States Army. Others with Montenero roots lived in other countries and served in the Great War. One who settled in Chicago received his United States citizenship by volunteering to serve in the US Army.

I talk with locals and learn that there are a few new stores in the village. These were created by returning soldiers who were injured during the war. The government does not provide pensions in such cases, but it does make a few jobs available so former soldiers can make a living. Crippled soldiers also have the option to run a government-sponsored store, called Salt and Tobacco. These stores sell government-controlled salt, tobacco, snuff, stamps, postcards, state document paper, school notebooks, and pencils.

Paolo Bonaminio was one of many soldiers who returned home from the war with crippling injuries. Like myself, he fought on the Karst Plateau. He and his family operate Salt and Tobacco Store #2. I ask him about his injuries, and he tells me about a dream. Saint Antonio appeared to him and told him to cover his eyes with both hands. Then the saint asked, "Paolo, what can you see?" Paolo of course replied, "Nothing!"

Then Saint Antonio told him to remove a hand from his left eye but to leave the right eye covered. He repeated the question again, "Now, what do you see?" Paolo responded, "Now I can see a little, but not very well." Saint Antonio told him, "Well then, you should be content." After the dream ended, Paolo immediately woke up.

The next day, in combat, an Austrian soldier

caught Paolo's right eye with a bayonet. Because of the dream, he was convinced that Saint Antonio had saved his other eye. Recently Paolo bore a son and named him Antonio in honor of the saint. He also built a small altar with a statue of Saint Antonio in his bedroom. Every day he lights a candle in front of the statue.

Ernesto Miraldi's story is like Paolo's. Both served on the Italian front in World War I and lost an eye in battle. Ernesto was a marksman in the infantry corps. In addition to the loss of an eye, he lost a leg due to severe wounds. For him and his family to make a living, they were given permission to start Salt and Tobacco Store #1. Ernesto is now unable to handle all the duties associated with the store because of pain and mobility issues. His father, Matia, and wife, Domenica, are running the store now.

After World War I the number of stores, cantinas, and restaurants increased. There are six cantinas where customers usually play cards while drinking some wine with food. Giovanni Orlando runs one of the cantinas. Matilde Procario serves food and drink at her cantina. There is a grocery store owned by Pasquale Pede. Terenza Scalzitti's cantina also has a room to rent. Quintino Zuchegna operates a grocery store close to the piazza, while Chiara's cantina and grocery store is in the piazza. Near the mother church, Florideo Iacabozzi has a store called the "Piccizeria." Rinaldo Freda runs an "after work" where people can purchase some grocery items as well as enjoy an evening of drink and cards. These and other establishments are convenient for the postwar population, primarily for the hardworking, hard-drinking men. I enjoy their comradery.

Everyday life is a little better in Montenero now than before the war. We work as hard as ever, but now we have more places to relax and enjoy the company of others. Our main festivals of the year are dedicated to Saint Antonio and Saint Clemente. During these special days we really do eat, drink, and be merry!

Since I've missed the feast of Saint Antonio for the past seven years, this year's should be extra special. A Christian monk from the fourth century whose full name is Antonio Abate, he's the patron associated with animals and those involved in related work as breeders and butchers. Montenero—with its history of raising animals for meat, milk, eggs, and other products—shows special appreciation to the saint every January 17 with this celebration.

Today, January 16, we are preparing for the festival. I go to the village square to watch and participate. Children are passing through the streets ringing bells and singing "Saint Antonio's Day! Eat and drink!" Hearing the children's ruckus, all the locals come out of their homes to offer a wooden log to them. Kids are tying two or three logs together to drag them to the square where the adults are stacking the logs to form a large conical pyre.

While the kids are on the street, women are preparing a blessed flat oven-baked bread. The aroma from the baking bread filters through every street. Tomorrow the loaves will be distributed to the poor who come from the surrounding towns to Montenero to beg.

After midnight, a small fire is built, *ur fucarigl'*. Youngsters enjoy showing off by jumping over it. The next morning, with the help of *ur fucarigl'*, a huge bonfire is lit as the morning mass is in process. Right after the solemn mass, a polychrome statue of Saint Antonio is transported on a platform to the fires where the parish priest blesses it. All of us walk in a procession to invoke divine favor for all our animals—cows, sheep, horses, pigs, dogs—around the village.

Following the afternoon mass, youngsters gather in a house to dress up in costumes wearing face paint and then noisily parade around the village streets. When people hear them approach, bread and wine are given out for the evening celebration. A person dressed as a devil repeatedly passes by the bonfire with an entourage behind him pretending to attack the bystanders. In a euphoric atmosphere enhanced by drink, a lottery is made, and a lucky winner will get the well-fattened pig. Whoever wins must provide a piglet designated for the festival the following year.

The statue of Saint Antonio is carried to the bonfire, where the priest recites a prayer. Saint Antonio is invoked so that the animals are saved from all evils. The priest blesses the fire, all the people, and the domestic animals. The blessings are even sent from the square to the animals located in the distant pantano. At sunset my favorite part of the whole festival begins. All gather around the warmth of the bonfire to cook sausages, sing, and dance in the company of homestyle local wine.

Over the next months, village life continues as normal. There's much work in the fields during the spring. Milking cows is a daily chore. There's also the cutting of grains, threshing, and grinding to make flour. Some make wine and others make cheese. Vegetable gardens are tended. We barter among ourselves. There is never a shortage of work to do. So, the midsummer festival of our patron saint

is a welcome break.

Ever since I can remember, the most important festival to take place in the village every year is held in celebration of our patron saint, Saint Clemente. It lasts for three days. The main day is marked by a procession in and around the village, headed by the parish priest, an entourage carrying the statue of Saint Clemente, and of two other protectors, Saint Lucy and Saint Margaret. A stream of locals follows the lead, which is nearly the whole population of the village.

Today, the second Sunday in August, our family members fall into the procession line commencing from the mother church, Santa Maria of Loreto. Father Federico Santucci, several altar boys, and a cross-bearer lead the way dressed in their fine robes. We make our way to The Court at the top of the village, then zigzag around many streets eventually arriving

at the bottom road leading to the pantano. Father Santucci blesses all the churches, chapels, and homes we pass. He also blesses bedding blankets hung in front of the homes.

The walk around the village takes about three hours. As the procession comes to a stop, Father Santucci and Mayor Giovanni Orlando give speeches inspiring everyone to embody their Christian principles, be good citizens, and to offer daily praise to Saint Clemente.

On all three days, vendor stalls offer a variety of tasty fruits. Locals play traditional songs on string and horn instruments and a professional band entertains us in modern styles. There is even some opera being performed! My mamma joins in, sounding more like a rooster crowing, which draws laughter among our friends.

There are some men and boys trying to climb a waxed pole that stands about twenty feet in the air. I give it a try. With shouts of encouragement from the big crowd, I still can't make it halfway up. Giulio Caserta is the first to succeed. He seemed to be the most likely to do it, since he looks somewhat like a monkey.

The main streets in the village remain filled with people. They have dressed special for the festival, wearing their finest shoes, shirts, and dresses. Some men wear suits, even though everyone knows they are down-to-earth farmers, typical men of the land. Among the elders, the showy dress is an attempt to gain some recognition, as having a profitable year. For the younger generation, the apparel acts like peacock feathers in a flirtation ritual that sometimes works! The festival is an opportune time for matchmaking. It's a part-time job for many of the elderly ladies.

Every bar and cantina is filled. Men play *morra*, "to flash with the fingers," the hand game dating back to Roman times—whoever guesses the total number of fingers revealed by all players when they simultaneously open their hands scores a point. Morra, like the card games and bocci, usually includes winners and losers. They play for wine, beer, or money, which often highly charges the emotional antics of the participants.

Eating, drinking, singing, and chatting go on late into the night. The ruckus must keep the cows up late too. Saint Clemente's festival is a special time when all individuals in the village feel their common roots. Memories are made to be cherished, appreciating the hard work of others and the care of family and friends. Such a special day revolves around a holy person, our village patron saint. Now that I am older and more inquisitive, I ask Father Santucci and others what they know about the holy man.

They tell me that Saint Clemente was born into a rich Roman family at the end of the first century. He joined the Roman Legion and was promoted to the rank of officer. He was soon held in high esteem by military leaders, who made him commander of a legion. For this reason, those of us soldiers who returned from the Great War have a special bond with our patron saint.

Emperor Caligula had pronounced a law that stated, "Whoever is affiliated with the Christian religion will be killed and given as a meal to the lions." To find out what the new religion was all about, Clemente dressed up as a commoner to attend a meeting featuring a Christian orator. The orator and other Christians would gather in the catacombs of Rome to avoid the police or legions, and to attend masses.

After having attended many gatherings in the catacombs, Clemente converted to Catholicism and began helping the Christians with financial donations and by giving advice on how they could elude authorities. Eventually someone accused him of being a Christian and he was condemned to death by Emperor Caligula. He was executed, but he was not given to the lions because he was Roman.

Clemente's family reclaimed his body, embalmed it, and laid in it a crypt. In the mid-eighteenth century, Pope Pius VI proclaimed him a saint and martyr because his body remained miraculously preserved and because of the assistance he provided to Christians.

The Montenerese greatly desired to bring a saint's body to the village as relics were believed to possess divine powers to protect them from any potential disasters. A request was sent to the Vatican. Pope Pius VI honored the request, and the body of Saint Clemente was scheduled to be transferred to Montenero.

The saint's relics were transported with utmost respect and caution. His body was removed from the catacombs of Saint Callisto, near the Appian Way. It was among the largest and most important of the Roman catacombs, being the official cemetery of the Church of Rome. It is large enough to hold nearly a half million bodies, including the remains of sixteen popes and over fifty martyrs. Eventually the popes ordered the removal of sacred relics to the city churches. They did this for security reasons, fearing that Arabs would attack the city, desecrate the catacomb, and steal the holy relics.

The body of Saint Clemente was transported to Montenero as planned. The village's new patron saint arrived on June 6, 1776, to the welcome of hundreds of inhabitants, as well as religious and civil authorities. A great celebration was held in the parochial church of Santa Maria of Loreto. The polychrome marble altar on which the saint's body now rests was completed in 1777. Plants and sacred symbols can be seen in the decorative marble rails and supports. Since then, there has been an annual Feast of Saint Clemente the Martyr.

Saint Clemente's presence gives spiritual and psychological support to the people of the village, helping ease our way through daily struggles. He is the one villagers could go to when no one else can help: when the nobles abuse their positions, when bandits raid, when an epidemic strikes or an earthquake occurs. Praying to the martyr comes from the depths of the heart and soul.

Since returning from the war, I have been in Montenero for twenty-three months. Much has been accomplished working on the farm and tending the animals. Above all, I've spent enriching time with my parents and siblings. We've enjoyed working together and have had fun at festivals and leisure moments, like riding my aged Gaius in the pantano accompanied by my papa and Berardino. I see Clemente quickly growing up. For a six-year-old, he's a smart kid who always smiles like Papa.

I've done all I can here to be sure my family is doing well. Now I must "jump out the window," and cross the ocean again. I depart from the Montenero station on August 11 for Naples and will leave the next day for New York on the SS *San Giovanni*. Parting from the family and the village tests the soul.

chapter 7

As Long as There's Life, There's Hope
finché c'è vita, c'è speranza

It is a stifling day as I arrive in Erie on this Sunday evening, August 26, 1921. It seems high humidity follows me from Ellis Island and has only increased by the time I step off the train. Seeing my brother Pasquale once again waiting to greet me, I feel absolutely fine. After the long Atlantic voyage, carrying luggage, catching trains and buses, all resolves into a quiet sense of being just where I should be: at my new home in Pennsylvania.

It seems a miracle that Pasquale now has his own car. Back in Montenero there are only horses and donkeys. His car is a used 1918 Ford Model T. We arrive quickly at his home on West 18th Street where his wife, Maria, is preparing dinner. I had never met her before but do know her parents. She leads me right to baby Antoinette, their daughter who is now over two years old. For my first night here, Pasquale planned a quiet evening to let me clean up and relax. After I shower, the three of us lounge around the kitchen table, enjoying the food and conversation.

We eat slowly. Maria's made a salad of freshly picked items from a garden behind the house. There's handmade sausage from a Sicilian store down the street. The other items are homemade, including red wine, bread, and pasta with beans. Maria goes to sleep about 10 p.m., but Pasquale and I stay up after midnight talking. He took Monday off from work to help me settle. He will work the rest of the week, and I can get familiar with the area around his home.

Pasquale made one appointment for me at a manufacturing company. When I interview on that Thursday, I get hired for janitorial work. The pay is good, and the schedule is steady. I begin on Monday. There are options for employment at other companies, but I take this job just to start having some reliable income.

When my brother returns home from work, he suggests: "Hey, Michele, it's Friday evening. Would you like to go out to try an Erie-made beer called Koehler?" We clean up some, then head out the door. We walk for fifteen minutes and arrive at the Montenero Club. With both hands held high above his head, the bartender gestures and greets me with, "Welcome back to the Montenero Club, Michele!" Men turn in their seats, and I recognize some. They are all paisans from the old country. Pasquale introduces me to the men and the bartender, Guido Fabrizio. Guido shows me updates made on the first floor, including the kitchen area. Then he leads us up a stairway to the second-floor hall. There must be a hundred men sitting at long tables welcoming me to Erie and the Monty Club!

Pasquale arranged this surprise. Many old acquaintances are here: Colonna, Miraldi, Calvano, Donatucci, Caserta, Pallotto, Iacobucci, Scalzitti ... All are familiar surnames from the old village. This club is a mini-Montenero. Aquilino Orlando supplies much of the food to be soon set on the tables. Angelo DiFilippo starts playing some songs on his guitar and singing in our dialect. All this comes from my thoughtful brother.

The club was started as part of a national mutual aid society that helps immigrants from Montenero. In the heart of Erie's Little Italy, it is a comfortable place where people from our village can relax and socialize, sharing stories of the past as well as ideas for the future. Over the next few months, we come here often, and I learn more about every club member.

Over the year, one elderly gentleman I've come to know better than the others is Vincenzo Caserta. Pasquale would always invite him to join our table. I learn later that Pasquale had ulterior motives in doing so. Vincenzo arrived in Lorain, Ohio, back in 1900 when he was thirty years old. After he got settled in Erie, he could afford to bring his wife, Filomena, and three of four daughters to America. So, I keep hearing about his twin daughters, Lucia and Ginevra, who arrived last year from the village. Antony Orlando has his eyes on Ginevra and I find myself being nudged toward Lucia. She is attractive, very well-mannered, and five years younger than me. As a janitor, I just don't feel ready at this time in my life to approach the Caserta family to build a deeper relationship with Lucia.

Erie is a thriving town and new work is available for many immigrants, be they Italian, German, Polish, Irish, or from elsewhere. A good number of people from Molise are working in construction. A stroke of luck comes one evening at the Montenero Club when I get offered a job building homes and businesses. The pay and hours are better than cleaning work, but the labor will prove to be physically exhausting.

Living with Pasquale, we are both building up our bank accounts. He and Maria have another baby in August, named after our Papa Serafino, as promised after their first pregnancy was a stillbirth. We regularly send money and goods to our parents too. Pasquale is very occupied now supporting his own family. I look ahead and wonder when I will start my own.

Being single, I work hard and often volunteer to work overtime. On the job, I feel like one of the mules of Montenero, lugging and lifting piles of bricks from one location around the building sites. After eight hours work, my muscles are so fatigued that it's an effort to lift a cold bottle of beer. I think of my parents, siblings, and the future, and keep working and saving.

After a year doing back-breaking grunt work, I become an apprentice bricklayer. It's an art gradually learned. It's necessary to understand how to prepare the foundation, mark guides, mix the mortar, and trim bricks. In the end, the finished project must look good, in perfect alignment with a clean laying of cement between every brick. It's very satisfying to see the completed work and know your effort will help others for decades to come.

All of 1922 keeps me employed with work on the most momentous building: Saint Joseph's Home for Children on West 6th Street. It's five stories high with hundreds of rooms, including rooms for cooking, a cafeteria, gymnasium, church, and classrooms. The red brickwork is not simple straight lines but includes many arches and a blend with accent rows of white stone.

One day I go to deposit a check into my bank account, and I stop to ask a manager for details about starting my own business. Would it be possible for me, an immigrant who can barely speak any English, to get a loan? Because I had been regularly depositing money in the bank for a few years and show no debt, he said there is no problem getting a loan if the business plan is solid. I said I'd think about it and will decide later.

I discuss my plan with Pasquale and a few other Montenerese who have started their own businesses. Perhaps inspired by my mamma's bread making, my dream is to start a bakery. There is a building on 17th and Liberty Street that I could buy, and it only needs to be set up with the oven and essentials like a mixer, sheets, pans, racks, slicer, and refrigerator. Many in Little Italy would be customers, plus I could sell some loaves to stores and restaurants.

It will take months to get everything organized for the bakery, so I continue working as a bricklayer. Pasquale can't offer much help as he just had his third child in April, whom they named Gesomina. In that summer of 1924, I cease being a bricklayer and I find myself working every night at the oven. Every loaf of bread I visualize as a red brick. I'm building my own company. I buy a used Model TT, the Ford truck, to make deliveries. By having a vehicle, I can also use it to help others for additional income.

Is this the American dream? Pasquale and my parents are very proud of my accomplishments. I have built a stable, prospering life in Erie. And now, I'm often visiting the home of Vincent Caserta and getting to know his daughter Lucia much better. I'm thinking of proposing to her by the new year.

Lucia's birthday is on December 13, and we're invited to the Caserta household for cake and ice cream. While most are in the kitchen and dining room enjoying the dishes, I talk with Lucia in the front room about feeling settled in Erie with my work but looking forward to getting my own home. "Lucia, I would like you to be part of my home. Would you marry me?"

She looks stunned. Happily stunned. With a nod, she quietly says, "Yes, my love." We think it best to keep this news to ourselves until I talk with her parents. If she's unable to keep the news from her sister, Ginevra, then the whole city would know by tomorrow. Perhaps all of Montenero too!

A few days later, I go to the Caserta home again and knock on the door. I know Vincenzo would be home after work. Filomena looks between the window curtains of the door and sees it is me. "Come in! Come in, Michele!" Vincenzo enters the front room and asks me to sit with him in the kitchen. Filomena starts making coffee and brings out a dish of pizzelles and other cookies.

After fifteen minutes of small talk, I turn the topic to their lovely daughter, complimenting them on raising such a fine young woman, and how I respect the Caserta family. Not wishing to sound overly syrupy, I get straight to the point. "Mr. and Mrs. Caserta, I feel I know your daughter's heart very well and would like to propose to her. If you feel I am worthy, I would like your blessing."

While Filomena is about to explode trying to contain her joy, Vincenzo shakes my hand and gives me a hug. Filomena affirms, "We could not be happier than seeing you and Lucia married. We know how she cares for you and see how much you care for her. You certainly have our blessing." Vincenzo bends an eyebrow and says, "Thank you, young man! Finally, she'll be out of my hair! Soon you will get to know her bitchy side and I can finally enjoy peace at home!"

Filomena hits him on the back of his head with

a kitchen towel, but both are joyously laughing. "Of course, we feel both of you will be wonderful together. Both of you are understanding, patient, and hardworking. Let her and your family know that we approve wholeheartedly." I tell them I am eternally thankful for their support and return to Pasquale's.

After telling Pasquale of the marriage plans, the news does spread quickly around Erie. For months I keep receiving congratulations and best wishes. Lucia is nervously thinking ahead too. We are set to be married at Saint Paul's Roman Catholic Church on September 17, 1925. In the heart of Little Italy on

16th and Walnut Street, Saint Paul's is a five-minute walk from where Pasquale and I rent. We attend mass, funerals, and weddings there regularly, and even dinners and festivals. The Calabrese Reverend Louis Marino will officiate our wedding.

In his own amusing way, my brother tells me, "It's about time you marry, you old man! I already have a wife and three kids. Heck, you're thirty-two years old. You better get busy so I can be called *Uncle* Pat! I shouldn't remind you that the Sulmona confetti of almonds and sugar candy given at weddings are to remind the husband and wife of the bittersweetness of marriage." He ceases jesting and adds: "You know I'm happy for you, dear brother. Remember I'm always here for you and Lucia."

After the start of the new year, the months pass quickly. I'm working at the bakery about sixty hours per week. Besides that, people sometimes hire me to deliver coal to their homes or for other side jobs. One weekend in mid-July, two Sicilian brothers, surnamed Salamone, ask me to make a delivery late at night. I ask them about the driving distance and what I'd be hauling. They say the drive would be about one hundred miles total and I will see what to deliver when I arrive at the pickup address. I don't want to take the job, but the money offered is twice the usual pay. I leave my home at midnight and return home at dawn.

Lucia hears me return, raises up, and comes to the kitchen table where I'm sitting. When she sees me, she starts trembling. "Michele. You look sick! How come your face is so white? Your eyes aren't focusing well. What's the matter? How do you feel? You want a doctor?"

I can never explain the circumstances to her or to anyone else. In the silence of my mind, I can only think that I must never offer my service again. What was done was at gunpoint. I had no choice at the time. I tell Lucia, "I'll be fine. I just need to sleep." The next day is better, but I don't feel fine.

The latter half of the year is what I can call normal, without any major ups or downs. I am transitioning into married life quite well. The business income is good enough that I can purchase a thirty-year-old home on West 20th Street. The area is pleasant with kindly neighbors, mostly Italians, but some German, Irish, and others too. After we move in, we learn that Lucia is with child due in November. This is a joy for us to learn, only marred by news that my sweet Mamma Antonia had passed on October 7, 1926. I'm mad at the world for her death. She was only sixty-one. I want to believe the news is not true, but the hole in my soul tells me otherwise.

My sister Elvira has married and living in Chicago, so my papa has only his two youngest children at home now. God seems to have compensated my mamma's death with our first child due to be born a month later, whom we plan to name Philip.

By this month of December, it's clear that the business year was excellent. I'm producing more than five times the loaves of bread than the previous year. I employ two people to keep the production smooth and deliveries on time. Winter arrives and the outside temperature drops, which makes working around the ovens more comfortable.

One evening just before Christmas, as I am about to lock the bakery door at closing time, four men drive in front of the building in a new 1926 Chrysler and enter. They want to talk about working together and expanding the business. Wearing such dapper suits and driving that make of car, I thought that they must be very successful businessmen. The car must cost over $1,000, about five times what my Ford cost.

We sit in the office and the obvious speaker for the group, Mr. Magaddino, makes me an offer. "Mr. DiMarco, we admire how you have grown your business over the past few years. You must now have a large bill to pay for the increase of gas used for the baking. We'd like to double your monthly income, and we will do all the work. You don't even need to come to the bakery."

Bewildered, I quickly ask, "How is that possible? I know how to bake and I'm responsible for the employees."

"Well, Michele, the product we wish to produce, we know about. You don't. We want to make alcohol. You know about the government's prohibition laws? There is a nationwide ban on the sale and import of alcoholic drink, but everybody wants it. It's in high demand. Even policemen and politicians will turn an eye. They are our friends, so we can make and sell it. The use of gas for the distilling would not be noticed as out of the ordinary for a bakery. So, we give you two choices. You can either work with us or you can sell your business to us. We will give you one week to decide."

After they leave, it's as if blood has drained from my veins. All the past years have led to building this business. Now that it is successful, I must lose it? I first talk with Pasquale about this while his wife is breastfeeding their newest baby, Ernestine. We decide, for the safety of our families, that I should sell.

I will take their offer and return to being a bricklayer.

The eruptive life changes since selling the bakery opens my eyes to some of the underbelly of Erie. Since I stayed focused on my own family and business, I was unaware of the illegal nocturnal activities in this town. The Prohibition movement is motivated by a religious attitude against evils associated with alcohol. Since 1920 it made the sale and import of alcoholic beverages illegal, which only spawns the growth in unlawful production, transportation, sales, and consumption. They call it the "Roaring Twenties" for good reason.

A few years ago in Erie, a grand jury made a case against many in the city government, including the mayor. The investigation called on over one hundred witnesses to testify, with nearly half being from the police department. The only bug that stopped the mayor and others from being indicted was that the grand jury somehow included women. It was accepted practice that only males can serve, although there was no law against females participating. Because of this technicality—and no doubt political pressure— all charges were dismissed. The illegal activities are not just in Erie, but across America.

Organized crime has been nourished by Prohibition. The Italian Mafia is flourishing in this profitable bootlegging business. It's a black market that is often violent. I've learned that Erie is a transportation hub, especially running illicit liquor back and forth across the lake to Canada. At present, all the associated illegal activities are at a peak and still growing. The government has patrol boats that are in service to stop "rum runners" on the lake. The crooks are smart. Criminals put airplane engines in their boats and easily evade the slower government patrol boats.

Selling the bakery was a great misfortune as I lost steady work and a very good monthly income. At least I managed to build up savings in the bank. Working as a bricklayer again, I must follow orders from a foreman, it is strenuous labor, and the pay is standard. I do enjoy the freedom of a forty-hour workweek. I work on the vegetable garden in the backyard, make improvements around the house, and spend time with Lucia and our son Philip. Because I had time to study for the citizenship examination, I finally passed and became naturalized in July 1928.

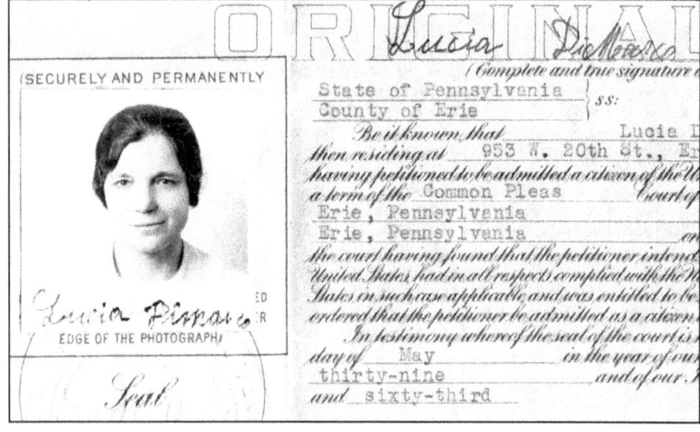

My dear wife is busy morning to night with the regular chores of cooking, cleaning, and doing laundry. It's major work taking care of little Philip. In January of 1929, Ralph, our second son, is born. Brother Pasquale now has four children with Vincent born a few weeks before Ralph. Pasquale and I have similar daily routines and both of us have been living comfortably during these recent years.

Now, nine months after Ralph was born, America and the world are hit with the Great Depression. Not only has the stock market crashed, but there is a downturn in all areas: industry, foreign trade, and income. It's a global crisis. I can't comprehend all the economic factors. All I know is that I lost $2,500 due to the financial impact, the average cost of living for a year. Plus, I lost my job. Construction work has come to a standstill, so I take a job as a utility man at Erie Forge and Steel. Each year for Christmas, the boys feel very happy to get some oranges in their stockings. We can't afford toys. My gift was getting my appendix out with five days recovery in the hospital.

We get by in our modest home. The garden I planted in the backyard provides food for the table. We preserve fruit and vegetables in glass jars for the winter months. Lucia uses a gas stove that is easy to light by opening the flow of gas and igniting it with a gadget that makes sparks. Because we don't have a hot water tank, sometimes we heat water on the stove for bathing and general cleaning. The coal furnace keeps the home bearable in the winter. If water spills on the floor, it turns to ice. In mid-winter, vapor from our breath is visible. Like most in the neighborhood, we don't have a telephone.

Lucia washes clothes by hand in one galvanized metal tub, rinses in another tub, then uses the wringer to squeeze out the water. She hangs clothes on a line in the backyard even in winter. Sometimes Lucia's close friends will stop by to help. They'll wash clothes or cook together, chatting to kill time and make the work more pleasant.

The family routine continues throughout the 1930s. When our third son, Dino, was born in April of 1933, America had started to recover from the Great Depression. Of course, we believe his grand arrival makes the world better, at least here in Erie. I can't keep up with my brother and Maria who have four more children, bringing their total to nine. We have a new neighbor too. My sister Elvira's first husband died in Chicago, so she remarried a man from Erie. Now, they only live one block away.

Even with her busy schedule, Lucia has been trying to study for the citizenship test. She has a wonderful tutor whom she admires greatly. Her classmates are all women from Southern Italy. They just took a group photo for their successful exams and are now naturalized citizens. Like I did, she had to "absolutely and entirely renounce" any allegiance to the Kingdom of Italy.

For Lucia and me, our focus remains on our children with the goal to bring them up with good moral character, to be healthy and educated. We want them to be able to read and write English without any problem. Since we mainly speak Italian at home, they must learn the language in grade school and high school. The boys help each other when necessary, but have friends their own ages too. The three sleep in the same bed and maintain a strict daily schedule while school is in session.

For grade school, our sons of course attend the redbrick Columbus School on West 16th Street in Little Italy. It was originally built in 1875 for the children of Italian immigrants. There are 418 seats available in the eight-room school. It's not the best environment for learning English. Most of the kids are speaking various Italian dialects while teachers are trying to teach them their ABCs.

Since Phil is the oldest, he is more fluent in our dialect than the other two boys. It does slow him down in learning English. Out of grade school, he now attends Roosevelt Middle School built in 1922, a grand two-story redbrick building on Raspberry Street. The school is full of students of mixed ethnicities where only English is spoken. One of our friends from Montenero, Anastasia Gasbarro, lives near school and saw Philip leaving school early. She tells us what happened.

"I thought it was strange to see Philip run as fast as his little legs would go toward your home. Odd too was that all other students were still in class. I yelled to him and asked if something is wrong. He said that he raised his hand in class three times to ask the teacher for permission to go to the bathroom, but each time she told him to put his hand down. Perhaps she knew he only speaks Italian and that she wouldn't understand him anyway. So, he decided to run home. He told me the reason."

While in full sprint, Philip shouts out in Italian, "*Voglio fare la caca!*—I want to poop!"

Oh, children of immigrant parents, how it is to grow up in America!

Heavy on our minds now is the possibility that our own sons may become soldiers. I fought six years in the Italian Army and now I'm a US citizen. So, in April of 1942 both my brother Pasquale and I are obligated to register for military service for America. Do you think we will be fighting Italians? My sons are still too young to serve in a war now, but who knows what comes in the following year or the next? For the time being, our lives are pleasingly conventional.

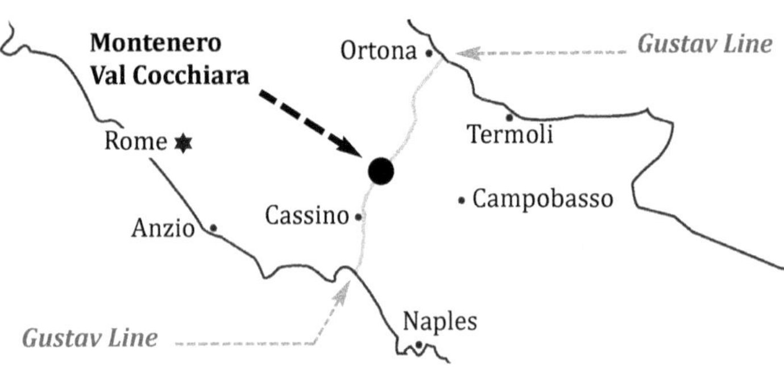
the
Gustav
Line
Montenero
Val Cocchiara
Gustav Line
Ortona
Termoli
Campobasso
Rome
Cassino
Anzio
Naples
Gustav Line

chapter 8

In the Wolf's Mouth
in bocca al lupo

War breaks out again, over there, in Europe in 1939. The Great War that I fought in—the war to end all wars—is now called World War I. This second World War may encompass even more of the globe than its predecessor. Although it started in Europe when Germany invaded Poland, other European powers quickly join in the frenzy. Then enter their allies. Germany, Italy, and other European countries have partners in Asia. To a few, it is not a total surprise that Japan attacked Pearl Harbor on December 7, 1941, drawing America into the conflict.

How will my relatives and fellow villagers get through this war? Will my American sons eventually be drafted and perhaps sent to Europe to fight Italians? Here in Erie, we gather the news however we can. It's a shame that the Italian-language newspaper stopped being printed here just a few years ago. So, we talk to people who know what is going on in the war. If they know English well enough, they read the *Erie Times-News* and listen to the radio. A few people have televisions. Letters are rare and slow in getting here from Italy.

In March of 1942, I did receive a telegram stating that my Papa Serafino passed away at the age of eighty-one. How fortunate I was to have him in my life. His death was natural. I'm thankful for that. After years of toil, may he rest in profound peace.

Montenero itself was relatively peaceful when my father died, but now I worry about my brothers. A few years prior, Berardino did military service in Ethiopia and has been home since. Clemente was not required to serve because he broke his back as a youngster when he fell off a chair. The accident stunted his growth. I'm relieved today that they aren't in the Italian Army. We are hearing news about its recent defeats in North Africa and in Russia. In the near future Montenero may not be safe either.

Since the earlier years of the war in Europe, we have become well aware of the tremendous destruction and deaths the Germans cause as they march across countries as rapid lightning, a *blitzkrieg* in Western Europe. But there are also major engagements on an Eastern front into Russia as well as a major conflict in the Pacific. Italy was allied with Germany and fighting against the US. As it did in World War I, Italy now changes sides. The Germans are not too happy about this and are treating Italians even worse than a regular enemy.

After marching through Sicily during the summer of 1943, Allied forces land on the Southern Italian boot. Composed mainly of Americans, Canadians, and British divisions, they have been battling their way northward. Hitler draws a defensive line south of Rome across Italy with the purpose of keeping the Eternal City under German control. It's called the Gustav Line and Montenero is in the middle of it.

By November 3, 1943, the Allied troops are standing face-to-face with German forces on the Gustav Line. The enemy's divisions are in place with their portable firearms, machine-gun emplacements, pillboxes, and artillery placements. Minefields and barbed wire are carefully placed to obstruct expected Allied charges. This makes a formidable force of 215,000 troops who are in the best positions along the line to defend against an oncoming Allied force that nearly triples the number of German troops. For me, much of this is reminiscent of the situation I experienced on the Isonzo.

When German troops first arrive in Montenero, some take over the most comfortable homes to live in. As months pass, the relationship sours, particularly after Italy joined the Allies. German troops are now keeping order through intimidation at the point of their gun barrels. Curfew is in effect.

The best observation post over the village is from the church's bell tower. A German machine gunner stationed there sees a man walking toward the pantano. The gunner shouts a warning, but the man doesn't flinch and keeps walking. The soldier fires and the man falls dead. This man was my cousin, Pietro Iacobozzi. He was a senior citizen, nearly deaf. He never heard the warning.

Another relative, Mariano DiMarco, is among those lined up to face a firing squad near the New Gate, *Porta Nova*, at the start of the street with the same name. Two men, Mariano and Alfredo Tornincasa, bolt for their lives. Mariano is shot in the back. His death leaves behind a widow to care for three boys and a girl. Alfredo suffers injuries and recovers. In the scuffle, the others are fortunate to escape.

Whenever a soldier is far from home and knows he may die any day, normal moral restraints can easily be lost. Villagers are abused in ways that are often too painful for them to describe. Using their bayonets, Germans cut off women's breasts. Italian women are often targets for rape. In Montenero, some hide in their homes, trembling as German soldiers pause on their doorsteps to smoke. They pray the soldiers will continue walking after finishing their cigarettes. In one incident, soldiers approach a young lady. The mother steps in to try to protect her daughter. Both are killed for resisting.

After living under such tyranny and seeing horrific acts of crime committed regularly, many locals leave Montenero seeking safety. When the Italian prime minister and fascist leader Mussolini is arrested, Italian soldiers become unsure which political side to support. One's fate hangs in the balance. Amelio Procario, a Montenerese soldier stationed in Rome, thought of a way out: he disguises himself as a woman and, with his purse under arm, makes his way to Greece.

Near Montenero's pantano, there is a cave where many hide while German soldiers are in the village. During the night, villagers sneak back to their homes and to hidden stashes to retrieve food. Under such tensions and conditions, it is not surprising that a young pregnant woman miscarries while in the cave. Shielded by the night's darkness to avoid being shot by the Germans, her courageous husband and his friend take the infant's swaddled body to the cemetery church to be left on the altar. It is all they can do.

As the Germans are preparing to retreat from Montenero, they rounded up whoever they could from the village to be transported to prison camps, such as one in Pescocostanzo. While Aristide DiMarco is being ported away by truck, he notices a thick brush by the roadside and jumps off the truck into it. Perfect timing keeps his escape from being noticed and he lives to tell the story. While in custody, he prayed to the Madonna, promising that if he escaped, he would name a child Maria in gratitude.

Pasquale Pede sends his young son Clemente to their stable in the pantano to save their horse. The young boy slips away and stays in the shelter for three days, alone and terrified, waiting for the others to join him. They finally arrive at the stable, as did a few others. From the stable, all could watch the village being engulfed in flames according to the enemy's scorch-earth tactics.

Dangers lurk in the village even after the Germans have left. One day an explosion suddenly breaks the relative calm. As soon as the blast is heard, my sister-in-law Ernesta Caserta runs to an open window screaming. It seems she instinctively knows that her son Antonio was killed by the explosive. He and four other children found a grenade, dropped it, and it detonated in Piazza Gigliotti. The same happened to other youngsters on Via Roma.

While children are playing soccer, they notice a local man approaching. He is holding a grenade that he just found. When the ball is kicked, young Ludovico DiFiore ran a distance to retrieve it. As he picks up the ball, he hears an explosion that kills his childhood friends, including his cousin Guerino Tornincasa. The boys were cut down in the flowering of their youth.

A seven-year-old boy finds a grenade in the yard next to his home. He is my nephew, little Ernesto Caserta. The grenade explodes in his hand, and he loses a few fingers. The Allies take him to Rionero, where he is treated in an American medical unit. To prevent any complications, the doctors decided to remove Ernesto's hand. A few months later he returns home. He will not be able to do much of the hard labor associated with village life.

All in Montenero who are on the Gustav Line, from newborn to elderly, suffer physical and mental scars from the war. The above accounts provide only a glimpse into the hardships they are facing during this period. The survivors persevere, some more successfully than others. Visions and memories of the horrors of war are often overbearing and can crush the human spirit. Or the experience can serve to inspire others to live their lives with purpose.

Personal communications have provided some details about the crisis in my home village. I have managed to gather several saddening reports of what has happened. From letters, telegrams, and phone calls we manage to learn about the fate of a few villagers. What I have not heard is also painful. I don't know if my brothers and other relatives are OK or not. Killed? In a prison camp? I just don't know for sure.

Troop movements can be followed by scanning the daily military news reports. Of course there is much coverage on other fronts too, but the Italians in Erie are most concerned about their homeland. We have a limited vision of how life is in the village with the German troops present. How and when will it change? The military reports parallel the personal reports. I'm somewhat fixated on following steps the Allies take as they approach the Gustav Line.

I become obsessive learning that the US and

British armies are poised near the village on high ground south of the Sangro River covering the road leading to the village. They are preparing to drive the enemy out with additional forces on the way. With each day, more villages near Montenero are coming under Allied control. On November 4, a British infantry unit enters Isernia. Five days later, Forlì del Sannio is taken. The British advance toward Alfedena and Castel di Sangro. Heavily defended, Alfedena is a strategic point along Highway 83, and the route through Montenero is the only route to the inner line of German defenses.

It is evident that whenever German soldiers withdraw from a town or village, they destroy everything and anything that could be useful to the Allies. This scorched-earth policy includes the buildings. In some cases, perhaps this is being done in revenge for Italy becoming an Allied member. Locals read evacuation notices to leave and know their homes will be destroyed on a specified day. The Germans are seizing all food stocks and cattle too.

For Montenero, November 6 is an exceedingly ominous day. The Germans announced that they will destroy the village, and all should leave. Some flee to other villages or into the countryside. The bombing leaves almost no home untouched. Even the gems of Montenero architecture are destroyed or damaged. Numerous villages are suffering the same consequences. I've heard that barely two walls of my parents' home remain standing.

While Montenero is being bombed, the British are planning a major attack along the east coast toward the city of Ortona. In hopes of distracting the Germans and thinning their defense in that area, they plan to

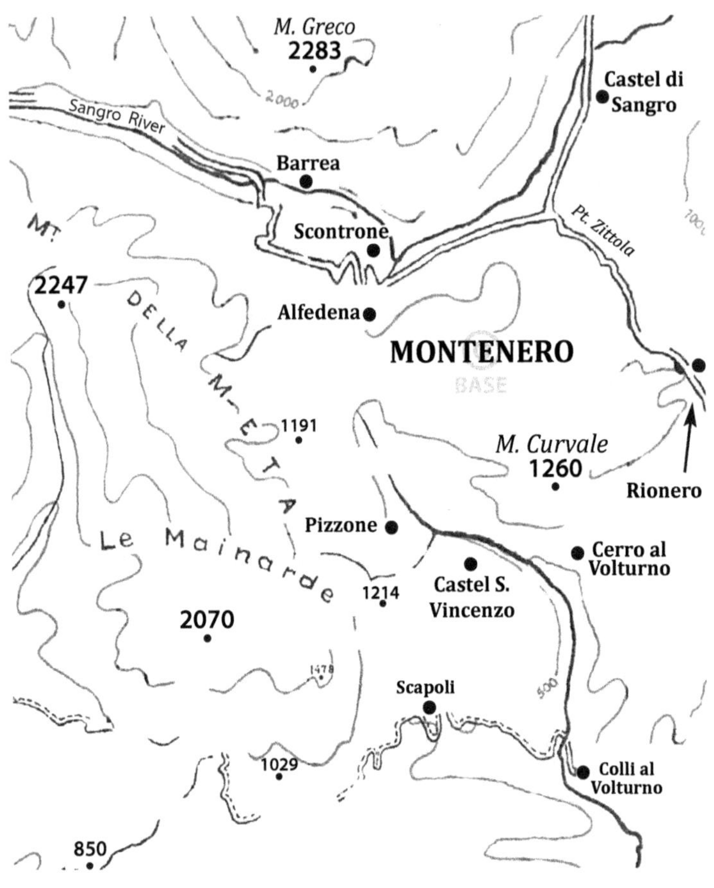

feint a major attack toward the Montenero area. On November 22, the enemy chooses to retreat, and the Allied troops move in and set up battalion headquarters in Montenero! On the same day, the British Army begins an offensive on the Sangro River. They reach Alfedena, a seven-mile walk north of Montenero and found that German troops had withdrawn.

During the cold winter months, Montenero feels the impact of the weather as well as troop movements along the line. Troops are arriving in and around the village. Most come by foot accompanying

Adapted from a Polish military topological map. Original shows Allied and German division positions. *Courtesy of Miroslaw Kucharski.*

Distances by road from Montenero:
- Barea 12.5 mi. 20.0 km
- Castel di Sangro 5.9 mi. 9.5 km
- Forli del Sannio 20.8 mi. 12.9 km
- Isernia 20.5 mi. 33.0 km
- Scontrone 13.0 mi. 21.0 km

donkeys porting supplies. Those under the British Army consist of a mix of Scottish, Irish, British, Belgian, and Polish. The prime duty for the Belgian and Polish troops is reconnaissance.

In late November enemy shellfire increases in intensity. The tracks leading from Rionero to Montenero by which supplies are being transported by donkeys are under heavy fire, causing dispersions and delays. However, the relief is completed on November 27. The total casualties of the battalion in this operation are four killed, twenty-five wounded and eleven missing.

Germans shell strategic points in and around Montenero and British troops hit targets with rounds of artillery and heavy mortars. There are deaths and some soldiers captured. The Allied presence in Montenero is bolstered when four South African officers arrive on December 2 and two days later another officer and eighty-six soldiers join the roster.

Early in December, the Canadian Division moves from Rionero to meet up with British troops in Castel di Sangro. Other troops soon arrive in the area to provide support. Under the British Army is a special commando unit. It consists of eight troops, mainly composed of foreigners. Three of the units are positioned in the Montenero area, including the exiled commandos from Belgium and Poland. These two troops are supported by a group known as X Troop, largely composed of German and Austrian Jews.

The primary mission of the Polish troop is to patrol the area and attack or disrupt the enemy where possible. Likewise, another Polish group conducts reconnaissance along nearly twenty-five miles of the Gustav Line, mainly on the strategic high ground of Montenero.

They are successful in attacking the railroad station in Alfedena and they weaken German defenses in the area south to Pizzone. The Carpathian Rifle Division holds its ground and provides safe travel over the roads connecting Alfedena, Castel San Vincenzo, and Rionero, including the intersection at the Zittola River. The roads are important to keep open for the transport of supplies. Soldiers patrol in armored cars in Montenero and hike to nearby hilltops toward Alfedena on reconnaissance missions. The enemy is nearby. On several occasions German troops sneak into Montenero and are repulsed by Polish troops.

The troops will never forget celebrating Christmas in Montenero. They divided duty and leisure with roughly half the troops celebrating on the 25th and the other half on the 27th. The soldiers have a wonderful feast that includes turkey, pork, pudding, oranges, tangerines, figs, and nuts. The meal is washed down with beer, wine, and whiskey. A piece of chocolate and a cigarette finish off the meals. The enemy could be heard singing "Silent Night" in the distance.

To help the Belgian commandos blend in with the snow-covered terrain, Montenero's parish priest provides white smocks that work as camouflage. Reconnaissance between Montenero and Alfedena is carried out in mid-February. An ambush destroys German defenses, and a few German lives are lost.

The Belgian and Polish troops welcome the London Irish Rifles, which arrive in Montenero in late December. In a thick blizzard, a German patrol is encountered, and firepower is directed toward them. But visibility is so bad that little could be seen of the effect of the fire or of casualties to the enemy. At night the snow accumulates reaching a depth of four feet.

On December 30 the London Irish Rifles, together with the Belgian troop, attack the Germans around Montenero. Such skirmishes with German troops occurred regularly. Fortunately, security around Montenero is strengthened when the London Irish Rifles of five hundred men take over the headquarters in the village on December 31. Troops are organized into companies and a battalion in and around the village. Three hundred are posted on surrounding hills, but about two hundred stay in the village. My brothers sleep in a barn, since soldiers have taken over many of the local homes.

The new year brings new operations. The Belgians participate alongside the Poles, conducting reconnaissance and dealing with the enemy. This group of commandos is composed of over one hundred men. One of the officers who helps form the unit is

Lieutenant Albert Deton. While leading a night patrol on a hill near Montenero on January 3, 1944, Deton is shot and killed.

In the early months of 1944, there are numerous encounters between the German and Allied forces along the Gustav Line in the Montenero sector. As the day dawns on January 19, two platoons are positioned in the snowy woods near Alfedena. They are hit with twenty shells, one being a direct hit on platoon headquarters. Only the commander is left uninjured. Troops jumped into their trenches for protection. Members of one platoon composed of thirteen men are killed or captured. Five men from the other platoon escape.

Other troops are called in and they counterattack with British artillery support, causing the enemy to retreat toward Barrea. The Germans take some prisoners. Following a shootout, the British prisoners are rescued. In all, the Allied troops suffer six killed, fourteen wounded, and nineteen are taken prisoner. The Germans have six killed, one wounded, and one taken prisoner, with others who retreated possibly wounded.

A few times the Germans actually reenter Montenero, as on March 7, but in each case are soon repulsed. Between March 19 and April 20, they lose Montenero and Alfedena to Allied powers. Allied forces are now pushing the Germans north, past Cassino and past Rome. The fight continues to press the Nazis northward from the rest of Italy.

For all that has happened in Italy, the time proves more fortunate for my sons in America. Two came of age to serve in the post-World War II recovery in different parts of the world. Turning eighteen years of age, Philip enlists in the navy as a seaman. During his two years in the military, he sees the postwar ravage in Okinawa. He deals with supplies, sometimes letting local children "steal" food from the US storage center.

Ralph enlists in the army, serving from September 1950 to 1952. Good with electronics, he teaches others how to operate radios and switchboards while serving overseas in Germany. Before he went into the service, Ralph installed our first hot water storage tank, had a telephone installed, and bought a black-and-white television for us. Just after getting the telephone, we received a long-distance call. I wasn't home, but Ralph said it was a lady from Thessaloniki, Greece. She didn't leave a number for a return call. It must be *her* calling. Although thirty-five years have passed, Evangelina thinks about me.

Our youngest boy, Dino, not old enough to serve, enrolled at Gannon College. He has a broad range of interests and likes to read.

Following World War II, peace returns to much of the world and to Erie, Pennsylvania. I had worked at the Erie Forge and Steel Company for over ten years. During World War I they were producing gun forgings and destroyer shafts for the US Navy. After my seven years with Keiser Aluminum, I finally retire. This year, 1959, marks my thirty-eighth year in America. It is a joyous time to relax and enjoy seeing my family enter a much better world than the old village where I was born.

chapter 9

Blood of My Blood
sangue del mio sangue

The war left Italy in wreckage. It may take another decade or two for the country to recover. The heart of American compassion and generosity shone brightly when President Truman created an economic recovery program to help Western European countries. Known as the Marshall Plan, it provides billions of dollars in aid. As America does this, my brother Pasquale and I try to help our two brothers in Montenero. Thank God they were uninjured during wartime. However, their homes and living conditions remain dreadful.

Right after the war, Pasquale bought a home on Brown Avenue to accommodate his large family. It's a ten-minute walk from my house. Three or four times a year we select items to send to our brothers in Montenero, such as quality shoes, clothing, and cloth. Berardino, his wife, Dianna, and ten-year-old son, Carmine, could use clothes and some household goods. Clemente too, but since he started his own tailor shop, we also send him cloth and clothing that could be altered for his customers.

I walk to my brother's home and enter. "Pasquale, I have some clothes that my sons outgrew. You can add them to the bundle for shipping."

"OK, Michele. I have a few more items to add too. These nice leather dress shoes and a warm wool sweater were left on the steps that lead to the second floor. My daughter Alice must have left them there to give to Berardino's wife."

We work together to bundle up two large burlap bags, sew them secure, and add the shipping address. Erie's main post office is not far away and easy to arrange the shipping. It may take two or three months for the bags to arrive in Montenero.

When we return to Pasquale's home and chat over a coffee, his daughter Alice asks, "Hey Pa? Did you see my new shoes and sweater I purchased this morning from the Boston Store? I set them on the steps."

I look at Pasquale's face and he looks at mine. Yes, we know. Yes, we sent her new purchases to Italy. Pasquale apologies. "Sorry, dear Alice. I sent them to Italy by mistake. I will buy you new shoes and a sweater." Alice just shrugs her shoulders. She's used to such happenings in the sometimes chaotic household of many siblings, relatives, and friends. "OK, Pa," she responds with a forced stern look, while pointing at him to bargain, "make it two pairs of shoes and a sweater."

I save every postcard and letter received from Montenero. There are a few classic postcards of the village. Some were colored by hand. There's a photograph of brother Berardino in military uniform taken when he served in the Second Italo-Ethiopian War. Brother Clemente writes to us more often than anyone else in the village. My two other brothers in Argentina, Carmine and Filippo, are never heard from again. We've tried to find them through the Red Cross and other means, but all efforts failed.

In recent years, Father Don Pasquale DiFilippo,

the priest from Montenero, has been visiting Montenerese who live in the USA, Canada, and France. He gives blessings during masses in our churches. In conversations, he shares many details about the village and how the people are faring. Almost every home there now has plumbing and electricity! During his visits, we receive the most recent church newsletter and some holy cards with an image of Saint Clemente on one side. As expected, he also hints for donations, which we gladly give for good causes.

I heard a big boost for Montenero has been what they call Rodeo Pentro. It started in 1974 and has been an annual festival exhibiting the rare horse breed and other horses. They gallop at full speed across the pantano. Montenero cowboys try their best to get on the backs of the wild horses to ride but are usually thrown off. Vendors sell drinks, sausage sandwiches, and more. Italian and foreign tourists attend. Erieites who have visited during the summer months say all this is great entertainment, bringing fame to the village as well as some extra income.

Although we think of our brothers in Italy, here in Erie we have much that demands our attention. My wife's brother, Oreste, has immigrated with his family. We've helped them at times, but they are very self-reliant. They purchased a home on West 20th Street about a ten-minute walk from our home. His wife, Elia, and five children have all adapted well. Their eldest, Ernesto, is the one who lost his hand during the war. He's not skilled with a shovel or pick, but he's excelling in academics! He received a degree from Gannon College here in Erie and will soon be leaving to study at Tulane University for a master's degree.

Oreste's home in Montenero had some damage from the 1984 earthquake. The large Mannarelli building that was once used as a hospital also had major damage, especially to its famous archway. Many people lived in trailers parked around the village until their homes were repaired and safe to live in again. At least there were no deaths as when sixteen Montenerese died in an 1879 earthquake. It occurred during their annual transhumance when they were taking sheep to Foggia to graze during the winter. The inn where they were staying collapsed.

Now we have a large DiMarco-Caserta clan in Erie that is growing rapidly. Pasquale's nine children and my three, plus Lucia's siblings have a total of eleven children. I shouldn't call them children because most are now married with their own children.

My son Ralph married Janet Balchunas in 1949. Her grandparents are of Lithuanian and Slovak ancestry. After Ralph was honorably discharged, he went to work in a plastic molding company and recently became their director of sales and marketing. He was given leave to be home when his daughter Sandy was born in 1950. Three years later, when Ralph and Janet have a son, they name him after Grandpa!

My eldest son, Philip, then married Carol Weber. Her family has roots in Germany. He has stable work at Erie Forge and Steel. Their son's name is also Philip.

After a few years attending Gannon College, Dino married Mary Ellen Donikowski and they have a son named Daniel. Her parents are of Polish background. Dino was involved in a restaurant business, but eventually went to work for the Soldiers and Sailers Home as their purchasing agent. Philip's and Dino's sons were both born in 1964.

I guess my three sons have learned English well enough to marry girls of non-Italian origin! The Italian, Polish, German, and Slavic mix of cultures are our contribution to the American melting pot. I'm very proud of them, their success at work and for making comfortable homes for their families. With them, there's never a dull moment when we gather. On most Sundays all of us meet here for dinner. On the major holidays, the immediate family is joined by many other relatives as well.

Lucia's kitchen is equipped with the common modern appliances. There is a hand-painted ceramic on the wall with a household prayer in Italian. She uses only one brand of olive oil imported from Italy, a special ingredient for the taste buds that no other oil seems to satisfy. Blocks of cheese are always grated by hand. Coffee beans come to life in the air, drawing one to the table to share both drink and conversation.

From the stovetop, oven, or broiler, whatever Lucia makes bursts with flavors that remind me of my mamma's cooking. Quality food is the priority for our family and friends. All the grocery shopping is done at the Brown Avenue Food Market, run by owners who have family origins in the village of Rocca Pia, not far from Montenero.

We have visitors almost daily. As soon as they enter the door, they know at a minimum an assortment of cookies and coffee will be served. The kitchen table's black-and-white enameled surface displays a vine and grape pattern. Over it are shared food and drink, but more importantly, the conversations. The kitchen—the campfire of our paleolithic man and the traditional hearth of the home—is our sacred space to share our intimate thoughts and feelings. For large gatherings, the dining and living rooms can fill to capacity.

At the recent family Christmas gathering, my granddaughter Sandy receives a gift that ignites her creative talents. After opening the box, she works continuously until finishing a highly colorful paint-by-numbers oil painting of roses. The fresh pigments glisten with brilliant hues of pinks, reds, and whites on the small canvas. Following the holiday dinner, the living room fills with relatives. Sandy finds it an opportune time to show off her masterpiece. After all politely praised her work, she leaves the painting on a small footstool, which everyone soon forgets about. As the group returns to their adult discussions, I sit down to share in the conversation, but soon get up to fetch a drink. While I'm walking toward the kitchen, everyone notices how realistic Sandy's vibrant flowers look—the wet paint clearly transferred upon the backside of my new dress pants. Dealing with my embarrassment is just part of having sweet, loveable grandchildren.

After Ralph got married, we turned our home into a duplex. He, Janet, Sandy, and Michael are living on the second floor. The children play in our spacious backyard with their friends. Originally, I planted the entire area with a wide variety of vegetables and some herbs. A peach tree was in front of the kitchen window. Now half of the yard is a green lawn that forms the play area.

When Philip gets married, Ralph purchases his own home on West 24th Street so the newlyweds could move into the cozy second-floor apartment. After Philip purchases a home on West 25th Street and moves there, my nephew Vincent Caserta and his new wife, Carmela, move in. No doubt, the apartment will become home to the next set of newlyweds in need.

We often encounter other Montenerese in the neighborhood—Aquilino Orlando's grocery store carries our favorite foods, Richard Donatucci provides produce to local businesses, his sister Rose makes a number of restaurants famous for her homestyle cooking, Antonio and Arturo DiFilippo provides nostalgic Italian themes in their music, Elmer Yacobozzi gives guitar lessons, Nello Fiorenzo sells and delivers laundry bleach to homes, the Narducci brothers tended to our dental and general health, the Ziroli brothers build and maintain our homes, realtor Rocco Orlando finds and sells our homes, and John Orlando Funeral Home puts us to rest.

We don't rely much on the grocery stores. Many items come from my garden of string beans, lettuce, fennel, zucchini, tomatoes, onions, garlic, carrots, parsley ... Sometimes I pack a large brown bag full of vegetables and walk to Pasquale's with thoughts for his eleven-member family. After I walk home, I repeat the packing process and walk to a son's, then another son's, with bags full of vegetables. I grow so many vegetables that I sell some items to the Brown Avenue Market to resell. Everyone at the store is surprised how I can grow such potent and unusually large garlic. They don't know that by tying the green tops into knots during their growing period, more energy goes into the bulbs.

Although I'm retired, thoughts of the family inspire Lucia and me to rise early in the morning. She cleans and cooks daily for me, the children, and grandchildren. Tending the garden consumes much of my time, especially the weeding. We don't need much for ourselves. We focus on helping others. I save all shapes of wood, lengths of wire, and pieces of pipe, to not waste anything that may prove useful later. Lucia keeps pieces of thread and rubber bands in abundance. Heck, she saves the keys that come with coffee cans, even though every new can comes with a key attached.

"A penny saved is a penny earned," as the proverb states. Lucia saves so she can leave a dime on the windowsill for our granddaughter Sandy, who retrieves it when she passes by on the way to grade school in the morning. Sandy could then buy some candy, and her mamma wouldn't know. She's getting a little chubby from Grandma's love.

I'm reminded of the recent trip I made to the dry cleaners to pick up three of Lucia's dresses. When I returned home, I set out the freshly pressed dresses across the bed. They looked brand-new. We had planned to go to Dino's for his son's first communion, so Lucia wanted to wear one of these flowery dresses. She tried on one. It felt tight. She tried on another. It too was too snug, as was the third. Her conclusion: "The cleaners shrunk all my dresses!" Her belt size had increased too.

Many came to visit Lucia on her sixty-fifth birthday. Somebody thought that a large, beautiful bouquet of flowers would be a wonderful gift. Lucia's all-too-truthful response? "Why you give me these? We can't eat them." Our family, like most Italians, value quality food above everything else except family itself. No doubt Lucia has a lingering sentiment from the old days in the village when a piece of bread was highly valued. That's how we old-timers are. Very practical.

Since Sandy started high school, she is there all day, including lunch at their cafeteria. Our grandson Mike is now in eighth grade. Since Ralph and Janet both work, he can't go home for lunch. So, Lucia is nominated to cook for him every weekday at noon. It's a fifteen-minute walk from the school on West 25th Street to her kitchen. After Grandma stuffs the little guy to bursting point, it is a challenge for him to walk the distance back to school. Unhooking his belt is of little help. Mike got smart. He starts telling Lucia that he just ate and doesn't want anything. She would still bring out the food and he could eat a comfortable amount without "hurting her feelings." Even while in college Mike stops for lunch and sometimes Ralph shows up from work during his lunch break. Occasionally their friends show up too. All know they will eat well. As Lucia washes the dishes, she is planning on what to cook the next day.

"Light"—that is the meaning of the name Lucia. My wife is the brightest light in my life. She is always caring, thinking more about me and the boys rather than about herself. She gives my life meaning. Gave me sons. Fills the home with love. It is at the end of our busy days that we can share time together, hold each other and express our deepest feelings. We often joke that we should put a cover over the statue of Saint Anthony that is above our bed.

There is a constant empathy between Lucia and me. Humor often connects our thoughts and keeps us positive. We show it in simple ways.

Mike and I are having soup at the kitchen table. While Lucia is at the stove, I ask:

"Hey, Mike, you like the soup?"

He answers, "It's delicious! I love it, Grandpa!"

"I'm glad you like it." Speaking proudly, I highlight that "I made it."

Lucia responds to the fib, turning to give me a stare. I just smile and her eyes twinkle. Jesting is a way to compliment her cooking and let her know I love her presence. I'm a lucky man, and not just for the soup.

Lucia rarely leaves the house, except to attend birthdays, holidays, weddings, and funerals. When she left Italy, there were no cars in Montenero. Sometimes she would ride on a donkey. On one occasion, my son Ralph comes to the house in his '57 Chevy to take us to a wedding. He opens the passenger side door to the back seat for Lucia to get in. She steps, not onto the car's floorboard, but onto the seat cushion, walks to the driver's side, then sits. Amazed, my daughter-in-law's jaw drops. For four-foot-ten-inch Lucia, this was just a logical way to take her seat.

A joy is when Lucia's friends visit her. Almost daily, somebody comes knocking at the door. Relatives of course come, friendly Montenerese, and others. Maria Jordano's presence always livens up the house. As an opera buff from Naples, she usually is singing *"Luuu chiii ahhh"* even before she arrives at the side entrance to our home. Her strong vocals add to her animated conversations, colored with Italian swear words we hope our grandchildren can't understand.

Mary Colona is another regular. Her demeanor is sweet and timid. She's always pleasant. She also makes Lucia laugh. From Montenero, they share common bonds and can talk about the old country and about the difficulties of adapting to America. Since they don't go out to shop or socialize much, their unique blend of Italian and English is a special dialect without a country.

From our house, Mary's home is about a twenty-minute walk for a young person. For someone in their seventies and eighties, the length of time doubles. After retirement, I sold my car and haven't driven since. I can walk almost everywhere I want to go. When convenient, Lucia will ask our grandson Mike to give Mary or others a ride home. To show appreciation, Mary would inevitably invite Mike in for something to eat like a sandwich or a pasta dish. In her polite way, she'd force him to drink some wine. Mike would return home a bit tipsy, but he'd thoroughly enjoy his visit and chat with Mary. Sixty years difference in age makes no difference in friendship.

Much has changed in our lives as I approach eighty years of age. A few of my better friends have passed—the old guys who made the Monty Club their second home. I'm blessed with my wife and brother Pasquale. I manage to see others I care deeply about, such as my brother-in-law Oreste and his family. They were especially attentive when I had cataract surgery and had to sit in my recliner for days with a large white patch over my eye.

Ralph stops by often and always helps maintain our home. He and Mike have put on a new roof, siding, paint, and generally watch for our needs. I do what I can in the garden and in the home. The garden is a meditative place. I look over all the plants while I puff on my stogie, appreciating the life before me in contrast to memories of the Isonzo. I enjoy giving a bag of fresh items to whoever comes by our home.

Mike also visits often. When he was very young, I'd take him to Oreste's home to get his hair cut.

Oreste bought shears and regularly cuts his sons' hair. Mike was thrilled when I taught him how to loudly whistle by angling two fingertips in his mouth on the tip of the tongue. It was a handy skill to have for signaling across the pantano in the old days. My skills at precisely plucking out small stones using a hoe in the garden were like magic to Mike, a skill equal to a pro golfer who could hit a hole-in-one at two hundred yards. I showed him how to shine shoes, how to use a broom tucked under the arm securely to sweep dirt into a dustpan, and how to roll an extension cord in loops by wrapping it around the hand and elbow.

One of our pastimes is playing checkers. I sit in my favorite chair, he sits on the floor, and the checkerboard is between us on a footstool. From that angle, he notices an Ace Bandage wrapped around my leg, showing slightly between my sock and pant leg. Mike asks, "Grandpa, how come you wear that bandage on your leg?" I point to my lower leg and say, "I was shot during the war long ago." Then I point to my thigh and to the other leg where I was also shot.

Ah, my poor little grandson. At eight years old, perhaps he is too young to know the truth about my wounds? He's never heard of World War I or any other war. All he only knew about wars was a little from television.

He wonders, "Grandpa, did you fight Indians?"

I explained, "No. It was in Italy, across the ocean, before I moved here, long before you were born."

Little Mike was in shock learning that his grandfather could become injured, shot so many times. He was also puzzled, wondering what the word *war* really means and how often wars occur.

The memory ports me back into a trench again

with the smell of gunpowder. Then I hear these words that bring me back to the present: "I love you, Grandpa. I don't want you to feel pain."

"Don't worry, Michelino," assuring him that I'm fine now. "I'm here with you today. Let's play chess. Don't let me win, like you did last time."

Years later, when Mike started college, he came home for the weekend. He was at our home when a small package arrived from the Italian Consulate General of Philadelphia. It contained a gold medal commemorating the *Fiftieth Anniversary of the Victory 1918–1968* in World War I. By this time, Mike had a fairly good idea of my military role.

Another medal that came is black with a multi-color ribbon: *Knight of the Order of Vittorio Veneto*. The fifth president of the Italian Republic, Giuseppe Saragat, had this created in 1968. These two medals were added to the bronze medal I received for the *Great War for Civilization 1914–1918*, which was given to the combatants of the Allied and Associated Nations.

These medals will go into my desk in the front room. Relatives know they are there, but the only people who will fully understand the significance they have for soldiers would have to have served on the front. The deep feelings of wartime can't be expressed in words. If anyone asks about the war days, it seems best to change the dialogue to another topic.

Mike and I also talked about Montenero, the garden, and other topics. Mike is the only one who asked me about the war and my escape from captivity. At the time, the practical skills I taught him and perhaps even the personal stories didn't seem so important. I thought the time shared together is what made the days so special. Much later I learned that the time together was made special *only* because of sharing personal history.

During Mike's college years, he went to India to study at Vivekananda College, part of the University of Madras. The day he departed, my wife saw me in my recliner chair with my head down. "Michele, are you crying? I have never seen you cry like this before. Seeing our grandson leave for a strange foreign land affects you so." Yes, in our mountain tradition we are raised to not show such emotions. It's considered unmanly.

I don't see my sons Philip and Dino as much as in previous years. I guess they are too busy with their own families and work obligations. Because Mike and Sandy are the oldest of the grandchildren, we know them well. Lucia and I don't really know the other six grandchildren very well and they don't know us. This is modern America in a modern world. Families are growing more and more apart.

chapter 10

Love and a Cough Cannot be Hidden
Lamoure e la toise non si Poisson nonsacred

The night's darkness is slowly giving way to the subtle shades of growing light. By habit, I've awakened at early dawn for over eighty years. No need for an alarm clock. A splash of cold water on the face and I'm fully awake. I shave, dress, and put a pot of coffee on the stovetop. When the coffee's rich aroma fills the air and is ready to be poured, Lucia will be awake.

I go outside, light a stogie and observe how the garden awakens to this day. Dew covers the plants, rolling off leaves. Seems the marigolds haven't deterred the rabbits partaking in some lettuce. It's early May and the string bean vines are reaching the post tops. I should pick some zucchini flowers before they close by noon and trap bees in their vibrant amber petals. Lucia can batter and fry a batch for lunch.

The mornings are always blissfully peaceful in the garden. From this vantage point, the world appears calm. It was the same in Montenero, at least in between wars. I visualize walking through the dawn mist toward the pantano. A slight chill is in the air. The fog hides most of the view, so only the path and nearby shrubs and trees are visible. As the sun starts to peak over the mountains, the temperature gradually rises, and the mist slowly clears. Roosters crow announcing that the day has begun.

Lucia sticks her head out the screen door and yells, "Michele! You're daydreaming and the coffee overflowed! What's the matter with you? You never remember to close off the gas before going outside!"

I finish my smoke and return to the kitchen. "Sorry, my dear. Without you, the house would burn to ashes. You are always there to finish whatever I start. You've prevented many potential disasters. You should receive a medal, or at least a big bear hug."

I sit at the table. Lucia gently places one hand on my shoulder as she pours a cup of coffee for me and for herself.

She proposes something for breakfast. "You want a frittata? Toast?"

Not feeling so well, I tell her, "No, thank you. My stomach is uncomfortable. I'll spade some of the garden and see how it is later. Maybe I'll feel better after some exercise."

I go into the garage to sharpen the knife I regularly use for cutting vegetables. It's a simple six-inch, hickory-handled knife that I've had for a few decades. When new, the steel blade was about two inches wide. It's been sharpened so many times it is only a quarter inch wide now. I walk through the garden, selecting a mixed bag of items to take to my brother's. It's too early to visit him now. I'll go sometime after 10 a.m.

I set the full bag on the garage steps and start spading a row of dirt. Pushing down on the shovel with my right foot, I feel a sharp pain shoot up my side. I try to ignore it, but each time I step on the shovel, the pain comes again and again. It seems to be getting worse, so I decide to go into the house to lie down on the couch and see if the pain goes away.

The discomfort keeps me from sleeping. When I move, the pain increases. By 11:00 I'm in a ball of agony. Lucia calls Ralph and asks him to come from his office during his lunch break. Maybe he'll know what medicine I can take for relief.

Ralph arrives about fifteen minutes before noon. He sees me curled up and perspiring and calmly says that we should go to be examined in the emergency room. I have trouble even trying to stand, so Ralph helps me get to his car. It's a Monday, May 7, and there are only a few people in the emergency room. I'm glad this isn't happening on a busy weekend. With only a few people in the waiting room, the doctor sees us quickly.

A doctor looks me over and asks many questions. But there are no solid answers as to what the actual problem could be. Gas? Appendix attack? He decides that I should be admitted to the hospital so they can run some tests and keep me under observation. I get X-rays, blood drawn, urine sample given. They give me some pills, the pain subsides, and I drift off to sleep.

I hear voices and awake, not knowing if it is day or night. I learn it is evening visiting hours. My three sons have arrived with their wives and my wife. They speak with the nurses, but there is no update on my status. We should know more by noon tomorrow. Doctor DiStefano, our family doctor, was born in Montenero. He will be able to explain everything in English and in our dialect.

Tuesday morning Dr. DiStefano looks over all the reports. They look clean. According to the test results, I'm in perfect shape. My sons are in my room pacing and waiting for some answers to why I'm still in pain. Their wives and my granddaughter Sandy are in the waiting room. Mike drove in from college to be here. I don't see the other grandchildren. Dr. DiStefano decides to do an exploratory surgery. By looking inside, he should be able to diagnose the ailment and hopefully find a solution. The operation will be performed this evening.

Lucia and sons spend the night in the waiting room. The surgery went fine. Dr. DiStefano said that the internal organs are functioning very well. What became clear is that scar tissue resulting from an appendectomy had grown around the intestines causing a blockage. Especially if the appendectomy was done slipshod, scar tissue can result over many years. DiStefano was the one who removed my appendix forty years ago.

The news brings great relief to the whole family. There is no major medical problem. The scar tissue was removed, and all the internal organs are normal. Now we feel it will only take some days for the area to heal from the surgery. Perhaps I can return home in a couple of days. This evening, it's wonderful to see my brother Pasquale, two of his daughters, brother-in-law Oreste and his son Vincent all come to visit. The grandchildren came today too. They are gathered in the waiting room, taking turns visiting in my room. I'm sorry, I am unable to speak to anyone with a ventilator tube down my throat.

The Thursday following the operation, the tube is removed. I am only allowed to drink some water. Nothing solid. I can't speak. My tongue and lips are so dry, they're flaking. I'm a little weaker on Friday, but I'm allowed to suck on ice chips. We expect to get an update from the doctor that I can eat soon. The nurses don't talk much, except that they are waiting for directions from the doctor. DiStefano was in surgery here at the hospital, but he hasn't come to my room yet.

Saturday and Sunday, there is no change, except I'm getting weaker still. No food. I don't feel like drinking any more water. I just rest with my eyes closed. Where is Dr. DiStefano? Shouldn't I be on soft foods by now? My family keeps discussing this, but no answers are provided. The nurse only checks my vital signs. They are still waiting for directions from the doctor. They say, "It is the weekend," implying that there is not a full staff present and some work doesn't get done until the following week. We wait.

Monday, May 12. I've been in the hospital one week. My sons arrive early in the morning to check on me. I'm weaker. My vital signs are slowing. Family members are anxious. The doctor hasn't shown up. Although my sons ask for help, it never comes. By evening many other family members arrive for visitation. I lay still. I can't move my limbs or open my eyes. I can only listen.

Some are optimistic. Others are not. Everyone is worried to various degrees. Other topics come into the conversations:

"I was supposed to play golf today but had to cancel to be here."

"I'm missing today's soap opera show."

"I'll practice more so I can do the backside three-sixty skateboard jump."

"If he dies, who gets the maple desk?"

"Can I leave now?"

Some comments please me:

"How can we help Lucia?"

"I always wanted to ask him about our Great Grandparents."

"I could not live without my husband."

"He would do anything for you."

"We should have visited Michele more often."

As I lie here, I no longer feel pain. I can't feel the operation site or even my lips that were blistering. I only feel conscious.

I call to mind the years in Montenero tilling the fields behind the plow and swinging the two-handed scythe under the blazing sun to harvest the hay. Thousands of horrifying images from the Italian front are still too vivid in my memory. To this day, leaving my parents to emigrate is still heart-wrenching. Working double shifts in dirty factories was part of my fate.

Could I have made better use of my time? I never wanted to waste it. Each hour and minute are gifts. They are special, miraculous moments of life. I have worked the land to put food on our table and on the tables of others. I've fought in battles hoping that humans will come to value peace. I've labored in shops and factories to give my parents, wife, and children a better life.

I'm sure I could have done better if fate would have allowed. I'm not highly educated and haven't inherited or amassed great wealth. I did the best I could each step along the way, including making my share of mistakes in the learning process.

In my family, we never had anyone graduate from college, until now. My sons and their families live in magnificent homes, drive cars, and have the modern conveniences only dreamed of in the past.

Unlike life in the small village of Montenero or the enclave of Erie's Little Italy, relatives now live far apart. The family bonds are very weak, even within individual families.

I value the feel of my wife's hand on my shoulder and the phone call from a grandson asking, "Grandpa, how are you?" Without being asked, my brother would show up to help me finish a construction project. My mother knew my favorite foods. My father taught me how to find joy in any kind of work and pleasure in producing fine results. These signs of affection give zest to life and make a life worth living. I'm thankful for those who have cared so much. Their loving expressions cannot be hidden.

What keeps a mother from tending her child, keeping it clean, fed, and nurtured? Doesn't she hear it cry? Why doesn't a friend bring cheer to another who is feeling gloomy? Perhaps it is simply a lack of compassion, being unable to feel empathy.

As my light dims, what now becomes of my family? Some said they should have visited me more often. Will they abandon my wife in her time of mourning, not making time to visit, leaving her alone in an empty house?

The day's light is slowly giving way to the subtle shades of growing darkness.

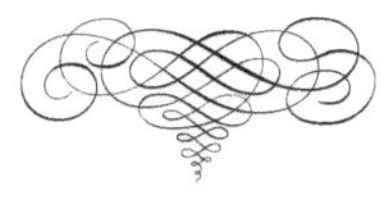

Epilogue

To give to the light—*dare alla luce*—is an exquisite Italian phrase in reference to childbirth. I've used it for the book's title as well as for the first chapter. Others may use the phrase to indicate taking some thing or a fact out of the dark and shining light on it. It is a presentation that others can see. Light is also a symbol for intelligence and illumination.

This biographical novella is based on the life of my grandfather, Michele Antonio DiMarco (1893–1975). In the story I am presenting people, places, and history with which I'm familiar. Much I can only guess! Much I'll never know. Real-life events form the story's structure. On it, I've entered a world of fantasy, creating some pigments to color in the missing segments of the portrayal of a life.

If you've read this book, you have met my grandfather and know his life experience and character. Many writers would think that the substance of his life is not of great value or interest. Michele is not an internationally known figure. An Erie street is not named after him. Many readers would think that his story is not very exciting and not worth the time to read. However, what would happen if the main character in this novella were to be replaced by any other immigrant?

By himself, my grandfather's life may not be so significant, but the life stories of all immigrants certainly have made and continue to make an enormous impact on the globe. There are many unsung heroes whose lives deserve to be recognized. This biographical novella should resonate with any person who has a story of immigration in their family.

One doesn't need to be an immigrant to have

such a compelling story. We see many whose very lives are dedicated to helping others. Their altruistic actions contrast greatly with the more common lifestyle of today's self-centered individual. Rather than work, there is play. Rather than be frugal and sacrificing, there is a striving for possession of "things."

The life of an immigrant, relative, or friend reflects their values that they hold most dear to heart. Hence, we have Mother Teresa and Al Capone—indicating quite a spectrum of possible characters! What we value reflects our own character. Since childhood, someone may have always had a dream of becoming a hitman. Do you know anyone like this? Others may focus on bringing laughter to their friends and family through their humor. Some are compassionate, donating money and time to the needy.

Do we have a choice on how our character develops? If we do, just how much can we nurture it by our own will? How much is influenced by our surroundings? A Chinese vignette entitled "Soot and Rouge" offers some guidance. Touch one and you become dirty and disgusting, but the other beautifies. Hence, we should be careful with whom we rub elbows.

I've praised my grandfather because he had praiseworthy traits. Many others do, but too often such people are ignored. They are old, pushed out of sight and out of mind. Their grandchildren probably know nothing of their lives. Their own children may know very little. Some heroes are laid-back and very self-effacing. If we make the time to get to know them, their lives can inspire in surprising ways. Of course there are some whose lives are not exemplary. Learning of their past can bring an understanding and some compassion for them and their faults.

Perhaps this little book will motivate readers to draw out the details of their parents, grandparents, and others in their lives. They may not have much more time to share with you. Their memories will not be on a backup hard drive to be retrieved at a later date.

Fifty years have gone by since my grandfather passed, but his name is still mentioned. His wife, Lucia, lived another eight years and his brother Pasquale for another ten. Sister Elvira lived another thirty-five years, passing six months before her 110th birthday.

The old house at 949 West 20th in Erie still stands in a now dilapidated neighborhood. The vegetable garden in the backyard got smaller and smaller as new occupants moved in. It has since disappeared. Saint Joseph's Home for Children on West 6th Street is as structurally sound and as beautiful as ever. It now serves as an apartment building for senior citizens.

Most of Michele's influence is not found in physical things. In varying degrees, his presence impacted family and friends. Yes, you can see it in the flesh as DNA passed to offspring evident in their physical appearance, especially facial features. Certain hand and facial gestures of great-grandchildren could remind you of him. In subtle ways, you could see his attitude emerge through others. For example, he valued substance more than appearance. The threadbare carpet in his living room was satisfactory for him. Rather than buy a new carpet, he'd give the savings to a son who could use it.

The guiding north star for him was a dedication to family. Because of it, he worked hard and shared his fortunes. Again, he's not a unique representative of this value system. Many others sacrificed as he did, cared for their families and had compassion for others. Every good person deserves praise. It doesn't matter what language they speak or in which culture they were born.

For a man who passed at age eighty-one, none would expect such a large attendance at his funeral. There were so many cars, flowers, and people, bystanders thought the city mayor had died. Many came in memory of how Grandpa touched their lives. Others came to give their respects to his wife, Lucia, and the three sons. I served as a pallbearer.

Growing up, it was expected that my sister and I would go to the funeral home for anyone our parents and grandparents knew. We'd have to dress and act properly for the occasion. Good chance my sis and I had no clue who we were going to see laid out surrounded by floral bouquets. But during visiting hours we did get to know some background of the person and their family. We also learned that there is a time limit on how long we breathe on this earth.

With the passing of decades, it became apparent that the number of people making time to attend funerals has decreased. When they do go, they may show up in their work clothes or sport uniform. Some parents simply tell their children that there is no need for them to go, thus further weakening familial bonds and cutting their vision from seeing the full cycle of life.

A great motive for me in writing this book is to encourage everyone who has gray-haired relatives to get to know their stories. Be nosey. Dive deep. They may surprise you with joyous and important tidbits. Their histories nourish our roots so healthy branches continue to grow. Let them inspire you so that, in the far future, a caring person will sit by your side to learn of your own story.

ILLUSTRATIONS

- PAGE FRONT MATTER: *Two Seated Italian Women with a Baby in a Cradle.* Charcoal artwork by Kristian Zahrtmann (1834–1912), dated 1889. The Metropolitan Museum of Art, accession number: 201529. Public Domain (CC0 1.0).
- PAGE 4: Village of Montenero Val Cocchiara. Photograph by the author.
- PAGE 10–11: Valley marshland (*pantano*) below Montenero Val Cocchiara. Photograph by Vincenzo Corona.
- PAGE 16: Castel Del Monte, Apulia, Italy. Photograph by venemama2. Courtesy of Depositphotos.com. ID: 62966209.
- PAGE 30–31: *The Immigrants* (1894). Painting by Raffaello Gambogi. Museo Civico Giovanni Fattori, Livorno, Italy. Public domain.
- PAGE 36: Horse in the valley below Montenero Val Cocchiara. Photograph by the author.
- PAGE 44: Michele DiMarco in military uniform. Author's archive.
- PAGE 65: Marble statue by Mars and Venus, by sculptor Antonio Canova, 1822. Photo by perseomedusa. Courtesy of Depositphotos.com. ID: 731047932.
- PAGE 86–87: Statue of Saint Clement. Photograph by the author. Procession of Saint Clement in 1948. Montenero V. Archive.
- PAGE 91: Passport photograph of Michele DiMarco. Author's archive.
- PAGE 92: Liberty Island photograph by Don Ramey Logan from Wikimedia Commons. CC-BY 4.0.
- PAGE 99: Wedding photograph of Lucia Caserta and Michele DiMarco. Author's archive.
- PAGE 104: Lucia Caserta DiMarco's citizenship document from the author's archive.
- PAGE 108: *The Red Bull in the Winter Line.* Painting by Donna Neary. US Government Printing Office. Pritzker Military Museum and Library.
- PAGE 116: Adapted from a Polish military topological map. Original shows Allied and German division positions. *Courtesy of Miroslaw Kucharski.*
- PAGE 122: Michele DiMarco and the author. Author's archive.
- PAGE 136: Woman with grocery bag. Photograph by nejron. Courtesy of Depositphotos.com. ID: 37395947.
- PAGE 142: Woman holding a teacup. Created by alfazetchronicles. Courtesy of 123rf.com. ID: 07604760.

ALSO BY MICHAEL DIMARCO

Mundunur: A Mountain Village Under the Spell of South Italy

Montenero Val Cocchiara (IS, Molise) is referred as Mundunur in the local dialect. Since Naples was the political and cultural heartbeat of south Italy, it sewed threads that tie Montenero to a heritage common to all living in the sunny south. 6x9 paperback, 334 pages, 222 illus.

READERS' COMMENTS

"An evocative, informative, and engaging study." • **Dr. Tommaso Astarita** - Georgetown University

"Its richness in detail distinguishes this substantial work of Michele DiMarco." • **Dr. Valeria Cocozza** University of Molise

"Enjoyable & informative." • **Dr. Ray LaVerghetta**, President, The Abruzzo and Molise Heritage Society, of Washington, D.C.

"*Mundunur* is a vital cornerstone in the small and growing collection of English-language writing on Abruzzo and Molise." • **National Italian American Foundation**, Washington, DC

"*Mundunur* successfully and comprehensively guides readers through the history, culture, and economy of Italy's Mezzogiorno." • **Quaderni d'Italianistic**a, Toronto

"*Mundunur* is an informative book about the past, present and future of Southern Italy and not just about the small village of Montenero written by one of its sons with love." • **Altreitalie,** Torino, Italy

"I have no reservation in recommending this book for Italophiles as well as community college and university libraries. • **Voices in American Italiana**, New York

English and Italian editions are available.
www.viamediapublishing.com

Did you enjoy reading

TO GIVE TO THE LIGHT?

This novella is about family life, surviving world wars, immigrating and adapting to a new culture. The main character is not a unique representative of this value system. Many others sacrificed as he did, cared for their families and had compassion for others. This book encourages everyone who has grey-haired relatives to get to know their stories, especially if they are immigrants. Their histories nourish our roots so healthy branches continue to grow. If you have benefited by reading this book, your honest feedback on Amazon would be appreciated.

To write a short review:

1) use your camera app
2) take a photo of the QR code below
3) a review page will open in your web browser

OR Visit **Amazon.com**, search *To Give to the Light,* and click on "Review this product."

Thank You Much!

Notes

www.ingramcontent.com/pod-product-compliance
Lightning Source LLC
Chambersburg PA
CBHW040828010826
48978CB00012BB/651